ALSO BY CARLY STEVENS

Tanyuin Academy Series

Firian Rising

Into the Unreal

Kingdoms on Fire

Tanyuin Academy Stories

Get a free short story when you sign up for Carly Stevens' newsletter!

Be the first to learn about new releases:

www.carly-stevens.com

LAERTES

A Hamlet Retelling

CARLY STEVENS

"Lord, we know what we are, but know not what we may be."
Hamlet Act 4, scene 5

CONTENTS

❧ I ❧
AUGUST

Across from me, Hamlet was a featureless monster clad in white. Sweat streamed down my back under the suit and slicked my gloved hand. A mask hid my face as well. I adjusted my grip on the foil. The room smelled of sour dust, the clatter and squeak of boots over smooth floor the only sound.

Hamlet lunged, a touch of aggression this time. I'd won twice before now, he the time before, and so on. We would not stop until he won again.

I licked salt from my lips and retreated, adjusting my path along the piste to throw him off balance. He might be the prince, but this was the only activity at which I exceled. If he wanted to create a rift between us, canceling twenty years of camaraderie, I could at least respond in kind. Perhaps I could make him follow and either get him out of bounds or make him look down, giving me a moment to strike.

The fencing master watched impassively, his limited praise reserved only for the prince who kept advancing as though time were slowing to a point that expanded and filled the room like an invisible balloon, forcing air from my lungs. Choking on breath, I caught a glimpse of eyeshine through the convex mesh of Hamlet's mask. The grace of an athlete became the grace of a predatory creature, the friend I knew disappearing behind a veneer of mad particulars: the shudder of a foot as it stepped, the rise of his chest too quick, the set of his shoulders up.

His foil flashed.

I parried, prepared to thrust, felt a jab to the ribs.

"A hit," declared the fencing master.

The gathered air dispelled in a sigh. I gripped the hilt of the foil, flexing my fingers hard against its surface. The glove fabric folded against the skin of my palm. I growled once, too late, in frustration.

Hamlet carelessly drew off his helmet, his dark hair messy, contrasting sharply against the whitewashed walls, the polished beige floor. He looked at me and his broad, resplendent smile held the venomous tilt of conquest.

One more. Call for one more. But he made it clear that practice was over.

I gritted my teeth, refusing to take off my own helmet. He would not get to see his triumph mirrored in my humiliation. He'd seen enough of that these past few weeks already.

Hamlet slashed his foil once in front of his body before turning to the fencing master to signal the end of practice.

The fencing master bowed his head—something he never did to me—and withdrew to retrieve cups of water.

Hamlet took his without a word and gulped it down. His wet skin shone red with exertion and relief at the victory. I kept my helmet on, though I took the drink offered to me.

Together, we retired to the next room to change and hang up equipment.

Hamlet leaned over the phonograph that sat atop a low table. The scratch of static sparked out of the slowly rotating record, and the first plinking notes of "Jeux d'eau" fell like droplets over us, quiet and gentle.

I hung up my weapon and finally hauled off my mask and hung it above, the effect like a ghost waiting for animation.

When I turned around, Hamlet had stripped to the waist and was toweling off his chest and face. I drank my water. We were both breathless from our bouts.

Accusations surged within me. My reputation unnecessarily sullied by someone who was the height of hypocrisy... Guilt of fearing that he was right... Fear of losing contact with one of the only people who knew me as a child... Anger on Elsa's behalf, since she suffered greater consequences than I for her choice... And a small voice that sounded a little like my mother saying I deserved whatever slander he hurled.

The clashing words canceled each other. No, I would choose to be the kind of man who demanded that another speak first when he had wronged me, even if that man was the prince.

Except for Ravel and the stormy conversation in my head, silence stretched.

I nearly shook with the self-imposed inability to speak, took another drink, eyed Hamlet. Normally, I could barely get out my thoughts when he was around. Even when we were children playing blindman's bluff, he wouldn't stop talking.

A knock interrupted our chance.

"Who's there?" Hamlet asked.

"A liegeman to the Dane," came a fruity, laughing, familiar voice. "Polonius, my lord."

My jaw squared. Hamlet and I locked eyes. His seemed to blame me for my father's indiscretion.

Instantly, my annoyance reverted back to Hamlet. My father, despite his bluster, had faithfully served the Danish crown and guided it through conflicts for years. I was allowed to feel mixed emotions toward him, but Hamlet needed to respect him for his age and service.

Soon enough, Hamlet himself would mount the throne. His brilliance and popularity would serve the country well, but I knew better than most how maddeningly unpredictable he could be. Would he go so far as to dismiss my father? Without Hamlet's goodwill, my family would have no recourse. So I reigned in every impulse I had and held my tongue.

I removed my gloves in marked silence.

"Let him in," Hamlet said, turning back toward the phonograph.

I obeyed.

My father bustled forward. He was all fine linen and hair product. Though gray at the temples, my father still had thick, light brown hair like mine. Every day, he tamed it so thoroughly that light bounced off his crown and made reflections on the wall.

"My lord," he began, then halted at the sight of Hamlet's bare back. He shouldn't have pretended to be abashed. We both knew he wasn't.

Hamlet turned only his head and raised an eyebrow.

"I'm afraid I have approached you at an inconvenient time," my father prevaricated. His ingratiating eyes finally found me. "Ah, did my son join you for your lesson?"

"Lord Hamlet joined me for *my* lesson," I corrected. "He insisted."

"Well done, my lord. *Mal seit de l'coer ki el' piz se cuardet!* if you'll forgive me," my father chuckled, his attention returning to the prince, the small bubble of discomfort broken.

Be damned the one who holds a weak heart and fears. A line from *Le Chanson de Roland*, a work I had recently studied in Paris.

The university called to me then, with its gilt books the color of chocolate and warm pastries, its bitter coffee and umbrellas in rain-covered streets, its pleasures and its company. The Sorbonne was another world with fantastical creatures that couldn't live inside the strict white confines of the Kronborg. My father, for instance, could never go to Paris.. His obsequious nature would be smothered by art and smoke and sharp minds. And I wanted to fly bird-like there.

"*Nus remeindrum en estal en la place,*" I answered, sullen. *We'll hold our ground; if they will meet us here.*

My father regarded me, faintly pleasant. He didn't know as much of the old poem as I did. Probably he had heard the rousing line he'd quoted somewhere and picked it up, shiny and out of place.

"What is it?" Hamlet asked, cutting through the meaningless chatter. He still stood rubbing his hands with the towel.

"Your father, my lord, is hosting a revel tonight in honor of the Queen's birthday and expects your company."

"I know," Hamlet replied idly.

"But of course you do. Your mother no doubt informed you?"

"Who else?" The prince and his mother spoke every day. "Is there more information I should know to prepare for this party?"

"It hearkens back to earlier days of Denmark's glory. Cannons will resound over the Sound." My father pasted a diplomatic smile on his face.

I'd never had that ability to dissemble. All my thoughts and emotions buzzed loudly just beneath the surface of my skin, no matter how I tried to hide them.

"Why, when I was younger," my father continued, "there was a similar gathering and people later surmised that the festivities could be heard all the way to Sweden and Norway." He laughed fondly at himself. "That was where I met... what was his name? The most accomplished Danish pianist, or violinist, since—"

"I assume we're invited too?" I interjected.

"Of course, yes." He didn't look at me. All his prattle was for the prince. "What shall I tell the King?"

"That I'm coming," Hamlet replied.

"Very good, my lord. I'll leave you to your leisure." He gave another chuckle, warm, inviting, hollow.

"I prefer *its* company," Hamlet murmured.

"Ah!" my father exclaimed, eyes rounding with delight. "Very good, my lord."

He paused awkwardly on the cusp of leaving. Was there a witty retort, a way he could bend a word further to his will? I saw the struggle on his face as he racked his brain. After a moment, he gave up, bowed as the fencing master had done, and excused himself.

"Tedious old fool," Hamlet muttered.

"I hope that I'm not *it*," I said, ignoring him.

"Should I have said *him?* Leisure, if anything, is a woman. You know that."

Heat rose in my face and I gritted my teeth before taking another sip of water. Ravel's splashing piano notes rang incongruously against my irritation.

Hamlet threw the towel to the side. When he looked back at me, he laughed. "You should see yourself, grimacing like an ape."

I closed my lips around my bared teeth. A certain level of flirtation and dalliance was generally accepted, though not talked about, but to go beyond that meant that I had become an undesirable, dangerous rake in the eyes of Danish society. All because Hamlet, handsome and well-loved, announced my indiscretion to everyone.

"Enough of this," he said. "No one in court cares anymore about your escapades. You're acting as though you've lost a limb when it was only a scion of your reputation." He hit me on the shoulder, brotherly.

The water left in my cup splashed, a few drops hurling to the floor.

Only. That was a deadly word. Hamlet couldn't know the power of *only.* That creeping sickness didn't attach itself to his name, just his sins.

"My reputation is tenuous enough as it is," I said.

"Yes, who is Laertes?" He leaned against the side table with the phonograph. "The wild one who likes new swords and new beds."

Not how I would have described myself. "Hamlet," I chastised.

But he wasn't finished. "A mini-advisor with everything but advice, a gentleman with everything but money, and a fencing prodigy with everything but skill." He leaned forward with the last accusation and winked.

I huffed an angry breath out my nose and began to change out of my uniform. "Lamord is a genius," I replied.

"That Parisian?"

Lamord was half the reason I went to Paris instead of Germany, where Hamlet studied. His fencing instruction was legendary. "Wait until the end of this year. You couldn't hope to beat me."

Hamlet smiled, at ease, as the song shifted. "I'm sure I could."

"He said I was becoming one of the best in France."

"That's not Denmark."

"That's better than Denmark."

His eyes clouded at that. "Don't add treasonous comments to your tenuous reputation."

But France was better. I could *feel* there, and didn't have to keep all my thoughts trapped behind my ribcage. Denmark, by comparison, was a prison.

I circled back again to my first grievance. My mind returned there often enough, gnawing on the injustice of it, wishing I could do something. "It's revenge, isn't it? That why you're doing this to me? You only talked to her! Do I need to keep track of each person you talk to?"

"Only those in whom I show an interest."

Hamlet, the notorious flirt. That would mean almost the same thing. Elsa, a wealthy businessman's daughter, had come to the last evening revel. I liked her, she liked me, I sometimes acted without thinking, and then Hamlet found us locked together in the Trumpeter's Tower.

"You didn't have an interest in her," I ventured.

He shrugged. "Isn't every act a sort of revenge against the boredom of the world? I could have liked her."

My father would have chuckled and gone along with this lunacy.

My sister would have gently sought to prove him wrong.

The King would have reprimanded his son for being too cavalier.

His mother would have defended him.

My friends back in Paris would have looked at me instead of him, a question in their eyes. *This is the prince?*

None of these reactions made it out. I simply blinked like a half-wit, voices circling like a school of fish in my mind. *I could have liked her.* The world belonged to him and he knew it. The truth of it made him inevitable as fate. Despite his protests about boredom, he was alive, alive, alive. People warmed to it, flitting close to him as if they could skim off some of his aliveness for themselves.

He slung on a loose white shirt. "Just wait. At the party, no one will remember. I'll be the sinner instead."

A breathy laugh escaped my mouth. Nothing could touch Hamlet. In his joviality or cruelty, he drew others to him as surely as lost children seek the light, even if the light was from a burning house. He could murder somebody and no one would hold it against him.

"Maybe we can both be sinners," I replied.

❦

Honey-scented candles twinkled in the chandeliers, illuminating the wooden ceiling and large paintings on the walls. The effect was intoxicating. Plates of *hors d'oeuvres*—pastry cups holding delicate cuts of game topped with bloody-looking blackberry sauce, the more modest *gravlax* with dill and mustard—circulated around the room. Conversation tittered in the air. Bright parrot feathers bloomed out of tall vases. Bubbles sparkled in glasses. Everything was meant to be reminiscent of earlier times when Kronborg Castle ruled the Sound.

The musicians played Niels Gade, relatively rousing and patriotic, but nothing like the loose jazz taking hold in Paris. Jazz had a freedom Denmark lacked. Or that I did.

I fiddled with the buttons of my leather suspenders. There was no use whining. I would return to Paris in five days. In the meantime, I might as well make the most of the party.

Elsa was nowhere to be seen, no doubt shunted into seclusion by relatives.

Instead, I spotted my sister. Her hair twisted into a style that looked intricate and loose at once, caught up and pinned at the base of her skull. Her dress had the same effect. It fell loose and sparkling to her heeled feet. She looked like a porcelain statue of herself.

I hadn't talked to her all day, so I strode up to where she stood speaking with a friend.

Upon seeing my approach, the young woman she'd been speaking to cast me an apprehensive glance and drifted away to mingle with others at the party. I tried to ignore her and turned my attention to Ophelia.

"I'm glad Father allowed you to come," I said. "How are you enjoying the party?"

She raised the champagne flute in her hand. "It's wonderful!" she exclaimed, then leaned forward to speak in my ear. "Lensgrevinde Katrine is here. You know I've wanted to meet her for a very long time."

"I remember you said something last week about it at supper." Against typical protocol, the two of us had eaten in my quarters that day. She had sat primly at a table, sewing after the food was gone, and I read a novel. Her company always soothed me.

"You know, she and her husband have two wolfhound dogs as well as a terrier?"

"I hadn't heard."

Ophelia took a dainty sip from her glass, her mood uncharacteristically iridescent. "I would love to meet them too."

A stir in the crowd alerted me to the royal family's entrance before I heard the announcement. A flourish of trumpets interrupted the music as they entered, creating a terrible cacophony. Unused to the event's unusual theme, the musicians paused a beat too late.

King Hamlet and Queen Gertrude entered, utterly resplendent in black and white—he in black, she in white. Their linked hands bobbed between them, maintaining soft contact.

The King's beard was grayer than I'd last seen. At the previous party, he arrived after I had left. Another massive *faux pas* on my part. I should have known better. I never should have gone to the tower with Elsa at all.

Beside me, Ophelia stirred. The milling guests parted and bowed as the royal couple maneuvered to a place of honor. They passed directly in front of us. The King's bright blue eyes never found me, but the Queen's did. She'd never said it, but I thought she felt a little motherly toward me. It was a greeting card type of care—warm from afar, sending me best wishes. But something in my chest constricted at the look.

Did she give everyone that smiling gaze? Did I just imagine it?

Only when they turned did I see Hamlet behind them. He wore black tails like his father's and an ironic twist of his lip that transformed into an easy smile like his mother's. His brown hair lay back against his head in a smooth parabolic sweep.

The royal family took their places in the general gaze before the enormous fireplace at one end of the hall and surveyed the crowd. I thought Hamlet's eyes fell on me for a beat. Just when things started to feel normal between us, there would come stark reminders that he was a prince, out of my star. We weren't friends as others were friends. Not like my roommates in Paris.

With an impossibly graceful gesture, Hamlet lifted a glass from a passing tray and hopped up on a wooden chair. There were a few scattered around the space nestled against wooden tables.

He flicked his glass with a fingernail and the Queen laughed delightedly. A smattering of applause filtered through the room. Without preamble, Hamlet began.

"I'm sure we can all rejoice that today we are celebrating a marvelous woman, one whose presence makes us forget about the weariness of life, the wars, the march of time." Hamlet's smile turned impish. "The law's delay, the insolent officers..."

Cries of protest rose from the dignitaries present. He quieted them with a hand.

"But seriously," he continued, twisting to lock eyes with his mother, "she is to be valued above rubies, as the Scripture says. Because of her, the King's kindness stands out in relief. He will not suffer the wind to visit her face too roughly."

The royal couple chuckled.

"No, it is true," Hamlet said as though they had protested. "He once ordered the clouds to stop blowing on my mother's behalf. Sickeningly endearing."

My smile was punctuated with the faintest bitterness.

The King squeezed his wife's hand.

"She is the moon to his sun, and we here in Denmark are lucky to have her light in the darkness." Hamlet raised his glass toward the crowd. "To Queen Gertrude!"

I scrambled for some champagne to echo his toast, but the nearest platter was too far to match his timing.

"To Queen Gertrude!" A hundred glittering flutes twinkled in the candlelight.

The King stepped forward as Hamlet jumped to the ground. The Queen embraced her son and whispered something in his ear.

"Music!" the King demanded with a smile, raising his hands in a magnanimous gesture.

The spell was broken. Everyone moved again.

"Laertes!" came a hushed voice from behind me.

I schooled my features.

"Yes, Father?" Where he'd come from, I didn't know.

Ophelia had floated away from my side. I spent a moment scanning the group for her. I felt strangely abandoned.

"Look at you," my father demanded.

I glanced down at myself. A crisp white dress shirt open at the neck, dark ironed trousers, leather suspenders, leather shoes. I hated bowties, and tended to get hot easily, so I avoided suit jackets. I could at least have worn a waistcoat, though.

I should have known this was coming.

My father's manicured eyebrows lowered, yet he still managed to smile like a showman at someone over my shoulder. "Your dress is a disgrace. You might as well be wearing one." A telltale glint crossed his face. "You'd best address the issue at once. Redress the scandalous choice not to wear so much as a coat." His lips twitched at his own cleverness. Then he seemed to inhabit his body again, temporarily abandoning the wordplay, though I knew it wouldn't be for long.

Nightdress... dress... dress... Hamlet would surely match him with a witty comment, but I couldn't anticipate the next jab. My muscles clenched as though it would be a physical hit.

"His Majesty is in audience." He puffed out his considerable chest. "Comport yourself like the noble you are and I won't have to dress you down again."

Dress down, of course.

Shame and defiance churned in my gut. My face went tight with heat. If I had worn a suit jacket, I might have exploded.

"Of course, Father," I replied, but I had no intention of changing. Denmark kept catching me only to find something wanting. A million little incidents clustered together, bunching in my chest. I set my teeth together hard. "I'm going outside."

He softened, releasing a sigh. "It's going to be a lovely night." He reached for the silver cigarette case in his breast pocket. The King himself had gotten it monogrammed PB in recognition of my father's faithful service to the crown. He offered me a cigarette.

"Thank you." I hurried to the far side of the room, where a door led out to a balcony and the slightly cooler air. The sun had only just set, the sky like spilled blue ink. Salt floated heavy through the humid air. I drew in a long breath through my nose. Another. I thumbed the cigarette in my hand, waiting for my riotous thoughts to settle.

A light breeze broke up the warmth and wove across my throat, a luxury I wouldn't have if I followed the damn formalities. I lit the cigarette.

The door behind me eased open. "Gone again so soon?"

Hamlet stood there. His presence simultaneously annoyed and comforted me. Who didn't want to be missed?

"I'm alone this time," I bit out, gesturing in a sweep with one hand before letting out a breath of smoke.

He seemed to take the movement as an invitation, whipping out a cigarette of his own. He put it in his mouth and leaned toward me. Automatically, I let him light his cigarette off the end of mine. No matter how bitter I felt toward him still, habit had given the movement a property of easiness.

We each leaned back against the railing. The tails of his black coat waved in the breeze like ineffectual wings. And in his buttonhole, not a flower, but a silk pocket square barely poking above the rim of the pocket. It was yellow, with the design of a small purple flower embroidered into it. The flower looked familiar, but I couldn't place it.

"I hate these parties," he said.

"You don't seem to."

"I don't hate them when I'm in them, but I hate to look at them before and after. Don't the French call you a drunk too because they've heard about these revels?"

They had. "Do they say that in Germany?"

"Not to my face. I overhear them. Once I sat beside a man and told him about how I put a snake in my tutor's bedroom after he spent a week teaching me diplomatic writing. 'As love between us like the palm might flourish, as peace still wears her wheaten garland...' As, as, as. I thought that drivel made *me* an ass. So I told him." He placed the cigarette in his lips again and drew. His father's signet ring sat heavy on his finger. "I meant to make myself look less of a prince. What that accomplished, I don't know, but I didn't hear him smear Denmark's name again after I'd smeared my own." He laughed mirthlessly.

I had no idea how to respond, so I just smoked.

"I'm looking forward to Wittenberg again," he mused, not looking at me now, "though I'll miss Helsingør. I can't imagine going without one or the other permanently."

"I thought you said Denmark was the paragon of nations."

He turned. "It is. But don't you ever want to escape your own body? You wouldn't flay yourself to do it. That doesn't mean you can't want more."

I did want more, but I wasn't sure how much more I could take. My mind was crowded as it was, all those loud voices vying for prominence. At least they muted somewhat in Paris. I belonged to myself in a way I couldn't here. Who my Paris self was, I couldn't say exactly, but perhaps once I found out, then I'd truly be my own man.

"It's our last year," I said, a heaviness settling over my limbs.

"One more year to fantasize about beating me in a duel."

"I can beat you in a duel."

"I don't need to add the word *can*. It's implied in the completed action."

The sky was darker and the moist air still stuck to my skin. To our right twinkled lights in the city of Helsingør. To our left was the still water of the Sound.

"Ah," he said, snuffing his cigarette, "who am I to crush your dreams? You're reasonably noble, no less than the rest of us. Come inside."

That meant amends. My shoulders relaxed and I followed him into the light.

In that short time, the air inside had grown headier with scent and bodies. Men and women spoke, the men in easy, charming tones and the women simpering in answer. Ophelia's voice—when she was relaxed, when she was with me—sounded nothing like her party voice. Was that true of other women too? I'd never had another female friend, so I couldn't say, but the likelihood presented itself forcefully to me. It was stupid never to have considered the idea before.

All the talking crowd that flirted and drank and danced didn't look toward me, as I suspected they might after the prince's slanders. More often I caught them glancing toward the sumptuous hangings by the fireplace where the King and Queen sat. Natural, I supposed. At a gathering that included royalty, who wouldn't comment on their presence?

The upbeat music shifted to a melancholy waltz, Tchaikovsky's "Valse Sentimentale". Hamlet asked someone near us to dance and the woman seemed enchanted to be singled out. Her blue eyes sparkled in the light of the chandeliers. They swept off along the checkered marble floor like a picture from a society magazine.

I disposed of my cigarette and asked the girl's companion. She obliged, but looked far less enchanted than Hamlet's partner had.

There was the effect of the rumors, rearing their heads like Hydra while I, like Hercules, could only avoid their teeth.

I placed my hand at the girl's waist, she placed hers on my shoulder, and our feet slid one two three to the rhythm of the song.

The King and Queen weren't dancing, though they had risen. The King spoke to my father, a florid smile on both their faces. Something loosened inside me. The Queen spoke to someone on her other side. For a moment I couldn't remember who he was. The King's brother, but what was his name?

"Excuse me," said the woman in my arms.

The fringe of her dress tickled the backs of my fingers where my hand had slipped to her hip. I corrected up to her waist again.

Her dewdrop lips curved into a demure smile and she dropped her eyes. "No, I meant to ask, what are you looking at, sir?"

"I..."

"Isn't it funny how the Queen keeps talking to Lord Claudius?"

Claudius. That was his name.

She kept her girlish voice quiet. "I heard from one of the Queen's chambermaids that she talks to him every day." Her lined eyes rounded at me.

"Oh."

"She didn't say what they talk about, but that seems funny to me. Every day."

I felt an odd desire to defend Hamlet's mother. "She talks to a lot of people."

"Every day."

I had to admit, that was surprising. The Queen spent her days either with the King or in her chambers, for the most part. She spoke with Hamlet often, but didn't have many other visitors that I knew about. Of course, I was gone months out of the year. The Queen was free to talk to whomever she liked.

"The King doesn't talk to him that often, and it's his brother!"

We glided past Hamlet and his happy dance partner. My girl wisely faded into silence within earshot of the prince.

So, Hamlet was right. Rumors had shifted away from me. This

party focused more on the Queen and her alleged escapades than my own.

The song ended, we thanked each other, and I found a glass of champagne.

Ophelia, across the room, drew my eye. She was standing in a group of men and women including, I suspected, Lensgrevinde Katrine. I headed there.

"Ophelia," I began before realizing she was listening to a story.

She cast me a blue-eyed look of admonition and I fell silent.

The fellow next to her, lanky with a red cummerbund, took a possessive partial step toward her when I approached. Apparently, he couldn't see our family resemblance. His eyes glossed with drink as he leaned toward her.

Ophelia giggled, but I was not so amused. At that moment, I was glad that I'd left my suit jacket in my room. It would have inhibited my movement if I had to push the man back. This goon wasn't good enough for Ophelia. He barely deserved to speak with her.

"I apologize to present company," the man said, continuing his story, "but this fellow and I simply came to blows over it."

Ophelia covered her mouth and rounded her eyes. "Oh, I can't believe it!" she exclaimed, taking on the trendy affectation in her voice.

"It's true," replied the man spaciously. "I can't abide a smear on the Holman name. But I left him groaning, let me assure you."

Then I saw that a woman accompanied the man flirting with Ophelia. She'd been nearly invisible behind him but now emerged to nod her agreement.

Ophelia lowered her voice conspiratorially, speaking to the woman, not the man. "If you could say the same, then there are bound to be no more accusations on that count, are there?"

Shock briefly registered on the man's face and his wife gasped.

"Ophelia!" I said, dragging her away from the little group to whisper fiercely in her ear. "You can't say things like that. I don't want people thinking..." *Thinking you're like me.* I had caused enough trouble already. I couldn't bear the idea of those same rumors of promiscuity following her too. She wouldn't recover. Her prospects would be destroyed.

"I was only fooling," she whispered back, tugging her arm out of my grasp. Her tone had lost the childish lisp, replaced with conciliatory one I was used to. Ever the peacemaker.

So where had that comment come from? Where had she even learned such things?

"I just..."

"It must have been the drink," she said. "I won't have another."

"Promise me."

She made the motion of turning a key above her heart, our signal ever since we were children. A smile played on her lips, at once mischievous and utterly innocent. I softened.

The night tripped along from there, sky turning black, drinks flowing freely, dance steps growing wilder, conversations less guarded, temperature rising with body heat. Cannons blasted over the water to cheers and applause. The ground shook, jolting our bones with each blast. The King called for more everything—cannons, drinks, food, dancing.

An hour or two later, I found myself near Hamlet again, this time in the far corner away from the fireplace where the King and Queen had sat. A group surrounded him as he invented a somewhat bawdy song to follow the tune of the music. I laughed along with the others.

Abruptly, he stopped. "Oh, yes. Monday morning?" he called, as though in midst of an ongoing conversation.

I turned. Ophelia had approached. Blurred with champagne, I wrapped an arm around her shoulders and drew her into our circle, though part of me knew this was no place for a lady.

"Monday morning," echoed one of the fellows around us, playing along.

"The perfect time for hawking. I'll see it done," Hamlet said. "Welcome, nymph, for you must be one, you look so lovely tonight." He dramatically kissed Ophelia's hand.

She blushed.

The champagne began to subside.

"Have you enjoyed the debauchery tonight?"

"For shame," she chided, her party voice intact. "There's no debauchery!"

Talking back to the prince. When had she gotten so bold? I stood a little nearer as though my proximity could shield her from any potential repercussions. Hamlet was a prince, and my friend, but I'd brain him before I'd allow him to hurt Ophelia in any way.

"Bacchanalian revel, then?" Hamlet goaded.

"Hardly better," she replied.

"It could be."

I felt sick. Flirting with everyone else was one thing. Flirting with Ophelia was different. A comment about the Queen almost passed my lips in retaliation, but I swallowed the words, instantly regretting the impulse.

"Maybe it could be," Ophelia conceded.

"It's getting late," I interjected.

"You'd be more correct to say how early it is." Hamlet's suit barely looked rumpled from hours of dancing.

"It's early, then. Come on, Ophelia. Let's get permission to leave."

"All right." There was an edge of frustration in her tone, but only I would notice it in this company.

I preferred not to talk to the King or Queen with trivial requests when I could help it, so we found our father, who teetered, expansive and bleary.

"Celebrations of this length are for the young people," he commented, "but you're quite right." He patted Ophelia's shoulder. "You have my blessing to go get some rest. Has Hamlet left too?"

"No, he's still here."

"Quite right. Quite right." He seemed to forget what he was saying, and turned to address the man behind him. An ambassador, I think, maybe to Poland.

As we walked back through the ballroom, the darkened windows blurred past. I paused and saw the wink of fireflies. Morning was near.

Glancing back at Ophelia, I suddenly remembered where I'd seen the purple flowers sewn into Hamlet's pocket square.

They were violets, Ophelia's favorite. She'd embroidered several items in her room with a similar pattern.

The silk scarf was from her.

❧ 2 ❧

SEPTEMBER

I'm not sure why I remember this day we played as children. Perhaps it was the timing, but it stands out sharply in my memory.

When Hamlet stopped spinning me, I held my arms out to steady myself. Thick fabric covered my eyes so thoroughly that I couldn't tell the direction of the setting sun.

"Laertes!" he called out.

I stumbled in Hamlet's direction, high-stepping to avoid hillocks of grass. The sound had come from just there. I swiped, hit air, and tilted, almost falling. Ralph and Gerrit—two of Hamlet's friends—laughed to my left. I whirled to meet them.

One of them let out a scream as he dodged. I was close, then.

Heedless of danger, I scrambled forward, meeting no one.

"Laertes can't tag us," I heard Hamlet say. "He has no more brains than my elbow."

Half-laughing, half-hurt, I flung my arm wide but missed again.

Giggles from Ralph and Gerrit.

"Pigeon-livered!" one of them cried.

"I would hit you," Hamlet teased, "but I don't want to infect my hands."

"I'm glad I'm blinded," came my retort. "I don't want to infect my eyes by staring at your face!"

"Ha!" he cried in delight. "Loathsome toad!"

"Toad!" echoed one of his friends.

"Frog," said the other. I never could tell the two of them apart.

I wanted to keep Hamlet talking, know where he was. "You all are worms and I'm a tiger," I said grandly, drawing myself up. My mother had read a tiger book to me and Ophelia last night, set in the land of India and full of heroes.

"Tiger nothing," Hamlet said from closer at hand. "My earwax is braver than you are."

An open-handed slap to the back of my head sent me sprawling.

I tugged off the blindfold to see Gerrit (or Ralph?) doubled over with laughter. The bright light glaring off the sea made me squint. Hamlet offered me a hand. As he heaved me to my feet, I purposely went limp so it would be harder for him.

"Earwax," I said, thinking and thinking of something clever to say, but all words left me. "You're earwax."

Hamlet laughed. "Okay, who was it?"

I pointed at the boy I thought was Ralph. Gerrit wouldn't be in such stitches otherwise. In the past, I always used to guess Hamlet, since he talked the most during the game, but he rarely hit me, so I was rarely right.

"No," said Gerrit, in a way that meant yes.

"Maybe," said Ralph coyly.

Gerrit whacked him with the back of his hand.

"Ouch!"

Hamlet ruffled my hair. At the time he was only seven or eight, but he felt older to me. "You're smarter than my elbow," he conceded. "Maybe you're as smart as my foot."

I screamed as we chased each other sans blindfold down to the water. Clouds wildly shaped like camels and whales swam overhead in a majestic sky. We played until the water turned black, and the clouds invisible.

🙳

I practically jogged down the Rue Saint-Honoré, bag in hand. Fashionable shops passed by on either side as I wove through the milling crowds. Late summer and a recent rain had melted the edges of the city, leaving it smelling of mold and wet stone and violet soap.

Many women liked violets. There was nothing to fear between Ophelia and Hamlet. A harmless flirtation, nothing more. Ophelia was a bright girl—brighter, I thought at times, than I. She wouldn't be taken in by his charms and his golden tongue and his power. Still, I expected a letter to arrive almost concurrently with me, perhaps on the very next steamboat, that would confirm that life at Kronborg Castle continued as it always had, without romantic developments progressing while I was gone.

I tried to dismiss that world and drink in this one. Multiple stories rose on either side, blocking out a vaster view of Paris. Here, wealthy patrons funneled through, shopping for hats or bracelets or perfume after a day at the Louvre.

I just wanted to get home to The Battlements.

Luc's chemist's shop marked a less desirable section of the famous street. I hooked right, the molded plaster façade giving way to pedestrian brick crisscrossed with a rusted lattice of fire escapes. Tilting against the wall out of sight of the street sat three metal bicycles: black, blue, and green.

Dirty water, remnants of the last rain, webbed the stones of the alley. Moisture seeped in through the seals in my shoes.

A rat, its tufts of fur sharpened into points by the wet, scurried along the wall toward the rear of the building. Bags of garbage leaned sluggishly against the stained red brick. The rat squeezed under a pile and disappeared.

The stairs shivered raindrops with each step as I clanged up the fire escape. The metal rail shone wet cold, slick under my hand. I pulled myself up, gripping my bag in one hand and the rail in the other.

Piano music grew louder the higher I ascended. One of my room-mates banged on the keys with all the vehemence of Beethoven or Berlioz in a bad mood.

Three stories up, a large young man sat on the landing, hunched over a book. The song thundered through the closed door behind him. His expression was a mystery obscured by his ever-present flat cap. At his side sat a small white porcelain cup with dark foam coating the inside and spilling over the edge. He clutched a small pencil in his thick fingers. Chalky gray notes filled the margins already. He'd been out here for a while, then.

He looked slowly up at me, deliberately closing his book—Cicero's *De Officiis* in the original Latin. Dark, intelligent eyes above a Turkish nose squinted up at me. He scowled, theatrical, then broke into a grin and stood to embrace me.

"Laertes, you bastard!"

"Julien!" I exclaimed. "How goes the world?"

"Not very well with that damned playing." He slammed his fist against the door three times. The music didn't abate. "Had to come out here to get anything done."

"But not the worst? Not the top of Fortune's cap nor the soles of her shoes."

"No." His eyes sparkled wickedly. "We live in the middle, at her waist. Or just below. Fortune always fucks with us. But we get by."

That was Julien Norgaard. Fluent in Latin, Greek, and profanity.

I gestured at the door. "How is his heart broken already?"

"He lives here all year round, you remember. Between us, this new girl looked identical to the last one. I swear to you there was no difference."

"Internally, maybe," I interjected, thinking of Ophelia, who was fine. She was definitely fine.

"Still no reason to play music like a demon from hell!" Julien bellowed in Danish toward the apartment.

"I need to get inside."

Julien crouched to retrieve his dirty cup from the iron grate at our feet, then stood resolutely in front of the door. "He doesn't deserve to know you're back," he scoffed.

"When did you get here?"

"As soon as I could. A week ago. My father had me working the business until the last minute." Julien's father ran a prosperous factory in Copenhagen.

"Let me in."

Julien seemed to grow. Even with a small coffee cup and a thin Latin book in his hands, his bull-necked, martial aspect came to his aid. The man could be terrifying when he wished.

"Move," I said.

"No."

"Damned doorkeeper," I laughed, and moved past him.

Piano notes crashed over me—big, angry chords. It was darker inside than it should have been at that time of day.

Julien leaned over me as he followed me inside. "Laertes!" he shouted, announcing me before switching to French. "He's back!"

The music cut off. Then there was a faint chord that resolved the raging melody, almost like a person talking to himself.

Julien and I forged deeper into the apartment until we emerged into the living room. Really, the entire space was storage for the shops below. I don't think it was ever meant to be lived in. A tatty piano sat against the far wall. All around it, cramming the room, were books, sketches pinned to the wall, small marble statuary on shelves, tennis racquets and fencing equipment leaning in corners, old mismatched armchairs, flowers on the desk.

There was a skull on the mantel, which I touched in a habitual gesture as I entered, smiling a little.

Henri Garnier jumped up from the piano. There was no sheet music on the stand. "Welcome back," he said, his soft voice at odds with the violent song that still rang in my ears. His blue eyes looked sunken and bruised but he gave a wan smile. His clipped black mustache rose with it. "How was your trip?"

"Long. It's good to see you. Has my luggage arrived? Any letters?"

"Not yet."

Julien high-stepped past us to the makeshift kitchen area tucked off to the left.

"You must be tired," said Henri, taking Julien's movement as a cue. "Let me get you something."

It was eleven thirty in the morning and I'd eaten no breakfast. I should have said *lunch*, or *nothing, thank you*. Instead, I said, "Pastries and a drink."

"Danish?" Henri teased.

"I can't change who I am."

"Getting it!" came a loud voice from the kitchen.

A moment later, Julien came back out into the living room with a tray piled with pastry and three delicate glass cups. In his other hand he held the neck of a green absinthe bottle.

I didn't bother going to my room. Setting my leather bag against a teetering stack of books, I took the offered glass and sank into my favorite armchair. It enveloped me in a familiar embrace. I slowly let out a sigh as Henri sat on the piano bench, and Julien took the other stuffed chair, pulling up an empty trunk between us to serve as a table for the tray.

"To our last year?" Henri suggested, raising both eyebrows along with his glass half-full of absinthe.

"Should that be depressing?" I asked. "It feels depressing."

"I don't want to be depressed together," Henri said, looking as though he were already sinking into that state.

Julien energized himself in response. "Then we won't." He lifted his cup. "*Nemo mortalium omnibus horis sapit.*" Then he knocked back half of what was in his glass.

None of the mortals are wise all the time.

"That's a terrible toast," Henri chided.

"But true," I said, taking a drink and feeling it burn down my throat. "To The Battlements!"

"The Battlements," said the other two together.

I reached for a pastry and smiled. I was home.

❧

My luggage arrived on time, but there was still no word from Ophelia. Images of her and Hamlet before he returned to Wittenberg —surely that was only a day or two behind my departure?—filled the darkness behind my eyelids. When would her letter come? Why had Hamlet been wearing her handkerchief? Was Hamlet attempting to seduce her in some misguided revenge against me?

The army of ghosts always whispering in my head spoke more and more loudly, more and more insistently, their logic bending like objects in water.

I wrote Ophelia and Hamlet separate letters but threw them both away, convinced they'd be irrelevant as soon as hers arrived.

By the time classes arrived, I was all but frantic. An overreaction, my father would say. My friends blessedly didn't notice, or, more likely, they did and left me to myself.

It was beautiful in Paris, the day classes started, and taking the bicycles out together for the first time was a ritual. Henri and Julien seemed happy, flush with anticipation.

As fourth year Classics students, all three of us had nearly identical schedules, so we rode together to the Sorbonne. Mine was the green bicycle, Henri's was blue, and Julien's was black. We wove through the congested morning rush alongside the Jardin de Tuileries, past the Louvre, and across the Seine to the university.

Julien stood on the pedals, one hand on his cap, as though he could see better that way. Henri looked earnest and took the corners fast. I struggled to sense the day around me, sucked down into my own worries.

Action was the only thing that helped when I got like this. I rode faster. Already, the early morning air was turning sticky with heat. The browning edges of summer were slipping into autumn but the days still peaked hot.

The Sorbonne welcomed us with its high white walls, stately as a monument. Its two great arms reached forward around the courtyard, closing us into its embrace.

I jumped off my bicycle a beat too soon and nearly tripped. My huffed breath turned into a laugh as I looked up and saw our Greek professor Dr. Lefèvre walking past us.

"Good morning!" I called almost hysterically.

"Good morning, Belleforest," Dr. Lefèvre replied more smoothly, almost as though he meant to calm me down. Ever since my first class with him last year, he'd pronounced my name the French way and now it was far too late to correct him. Really, the name sounded more pedestrian, like a bell in a forest, like the English would say it. Maybe in the mists of time, around the Battle of Hastings, my family's name had been pronounced like my professor said it. It didn't matter now.

Julien gave me a skeptical look when he caught up to me. Henri echoed the expression as we stowed our bicycles. I shrugged away my odd behavior, tripping up the flight of shallow stairs to the main entrance.

Our only class of the day was two hours of *Préparation Agrégation Lettres Classiques*, an intensive course preparing us for a competitive set of exams throughout the year. My studying had been uneven the past three years, so I had no idea whether or not I would be able to pass. Henri and Julien, though, were bound to succeed.

Nerves haunted me through the halls to the amphitheater. I quickened my pace, as though I could outrun my misgivings. The exam was months away.

And Ophelia was days away.

The paneled halls of the university normally set my blood on fire, providing proof that I was here in Paris where I belonged. The close air of academia filled my mind with fantasies of what I would do with my freedom. Thousands of years of knowledge and a world of possibilities—that was what the Sorbonne represented. That, and, more intimately, my friends. But today the building felt strange, as if it were loath to welcome me back. It was a creature that sensed my anxiety and drew back from it.

I inhaled deeply through my nose.

Hamlet will charm Ophelia. He charms everyone. She trusts everyone. They'll be drawn into each other's arms. He'll be found with her like you were found with Elsa. She'll be ruined. Or else he'll leave her and she'll feel devastated. How much is she like Mother? Have you ever bothered to find out, I berated myself, *to ask her questions that scare the marrow from your bones? She knows you, but do you know her?*

"Are we starting with Cicero? Do you know? I forgot to bring all my books," I said, my tone oddly breathless.

"I brought the extra copy by the door," Henri replied, handing me the slim volume.

I slipped it in my bag.

"Are you going to start like that again?" Julien asked me. He looked at Henri. "Don't coddle him."

"I'm not coddling him."

"He could have remembered it himself."

"I'm here and I have my own voice," I interjected.

Other young men pressed past us into the room. Fabric shifted and books thunked hollowly on desks as students took their places. The small amphitheater smelled like soft lead and wood polish. A mural splashed grandly behind the professor's podium.

Choosing a place toward the back, we took our seats along the long, curving bench. I sat between Henri, who had fallen back into the melancholy that gripped him in moments of quiet, and Julien, whose blunt face fairly glowed with appreciation as he took in the scene.

That first class is dappled in my memory. I can't remember much of what the professor said. Thankfully, he never called on me. To force apprehension from my mind, I stared at the painted mural. It showed a thick ridge of mountains plunging to the sea, or perhaps an enormous lake. The wooden frame around the chalkboard seemed to blend with the dusty road leading through sparse trees to the rock faces beyond. Did that mean that the professor himself was on a journey?

A sharp pain in my ribs made me refocus. Julien glared and raised his eyebrows. I bent over my notes again, which were woefully incomplete. I didn't bother to side-eye Julien's, since his were usually incomprehensible to the casual observer, always done in small cursive, usually with a dull pencil. Henri's writing looked neater. I copied his notes, pressing my pencil so hard my fingers had indentations by the end of class. I hadn't gotten much out of the lecture, but I had the notes and I would drown in the words of Cicero later tonight, letting them take over my roiling thoughts. I'd pin each Latin word to my mind like an insect to a board and examine it carefully. Words in black and white tended to pierce into my consciousness more easily than spoken words.

Julien left his book open for a beat as we packed to leave. I finally took the hint and looked, squinting at the scrawl. Not only had he apparently written down the lecture word for word, but he'd somehow also managed to write a dirty limerick in the margins. In Latin. Complete with the correct scansion. A dry chuckle escaped my throat.

Henri didn't bother looking. He must not have been in the mood for Julien's antics. "I'm going to the Moreau," he announced.

Neither of us was surprised. It was Henri's favorite place, apart from The Battlements. He went to the museum at least twice a week to study or, more often, to draw.

"I have Lamord," I said next. I'd stop by home and exchange school supplies for fencing equipment before my lesson. The idea soothed me as surely as a nightcap. Sport always calmed my nerves. And I could see if there was a letter at home. Surely, one would be waiting.

To indicate his plans, Julien tapped the cover of *De Officiis* with a thick forefinger. He didn't need to say he was aiming for highest marks on the examinations. We'd known since our first year.

Minutes later, black and green bicycles whizzed back through the streets. Julien didn't tell me to slow down, but the way he followed formed a question. There was irritation in the way he pulled up beside me and fell back. I ignored him. The sooner I got home, the sooner I'd get answers.

My bicycle slid to a halt beneath the fire escape alongside Luc's chemist shop. I charged around the corner. All our mail was left with Luc, who normally sent his assistant to drop it off. The Battlements were accessible from the inside of the shop, but we kept the door to the stairwell locked. Only Luc had the key and he respected his nephew Henri's privacy. Or he didn't care. Either way was a boon for us. The only exception was when he sent someone to drop off the mail and a piece was too thick to wedge under the door.

The chemist had black hair like Henri's, graying at the temples. His eyes were a shocking green. The first time I saw him, he reminded me of a self-portrait I'd seen of John Waterhouse. Appropriate, since Henri looked like most of the male subjects in Waterhouse's paintings.

Today, Luc wore a vest with many cunning pockets. Despite the family's wealth, he seemed to rotate through only three vests. All of them had spots of chemical discoloration. His knobby fingers looked splotchy at the ends. Once, he confided in me that he only used a mask and gloves to deal with two of the most lethal substances in his lab. He named them, but I'd never had a mind for chemistry. The rest, he assured me, he was careful enough to deal with on his own. His cleanly shaven face betrayed more times that the chemicals had gotten the better of him. Pockmarks dotted his cheeks. One notable scar gave his eyebrow a villainous lift.

Those piercing eyes met mine as I barreled into the shop. Tiny, meticulously labeled jars and drawers covered the walls and the counter. Delicate bunches of herbs lay in piles or hung suspended on hooks. An earthy yet antiseptic air permeated my lungs. I realized I was sweaty from my ride. I wiped moisture from my forehead with the back of my hand.

"Do I have a letter? Do I have any mail?"

Luc lifted his skewed eyebrow. "Do I look like the postman?" he grumbled.

The Battlements and the shop had an unspoken agreement not to bother one another. Friendly visits were acceptable, but I had breached the code.

"Please. I'm waiting for a letter. Do I have one?"

"No."

Blood pounded in my ears. "Do I have any mail at all? Has it come yet?"

"Save me a trip up," he said under his breath, handing me a thin stack of envelopes.

I rifled through the contents. Two for Julien, one for Henri, nothing for me.

Maybe I thanked him, but my mind was fiery again with worry.

When I turned around, Julien's large shape blocked my path. "Who's this damn letter from? Did you find someone special in Denmark?"

Without answering, I thrust the pile of letters into Julien's hands. He followed me around the corner and up to the stairs to The Battlements. Just past the threshold, paper fluttered as Julien threw the mail down. A big hand grabbed my shoulder, forcing me to turn.

"What's wrong?" he demanded. "You've been antsy as a cur in heat all day." He eased his bookbag off his shoulder and dumped it against the wall, his hand drifting automatically up to the skull. Rituals were hard to break.

"Nothing. Nothing."

"Fuck that. Liar."

I put my bag next to Julien's and gathered my fencing gear from the other side of the room. "I'm waiting to hear from my sister."

"Ophelia?" His brows knotted. "Is something wrong with her?"

"No. I don't know."

"Then why have you been crazy all day?"

"She might not be fine." For some reason, I didn't want to voice my concerns about her and Hamlet. Everyone loved Hamlet, from the fishermen to the society magazines. What if Julien laughed me off, called it lucky for her?

What if it was?

The idea made me pause. I'd assumed he had devious intentions, but what if Hamlet really liked her? What if he treated her well? What if he made Ophelia queen one day?

My thoughts tripped and fell there. Hamlet's will wasn't his own. The health of the whole state depended on him. He wouldn't marry someone who couldn't offer him power or money. Even if he liked Ophelia, he could never make her queen.

"Why wouldn't she be all right?" Julien asked.

"Because Hamlet's shown an interest in her." I never could close my mouth. I tucked a foil into its bag and zipped it up.

"*Hamlet* Hamlet? I assume the younger."

"Of course the younger. What do you think goes on at the castle?" But he'd managed to make me smile.

Regardless, I looked forward to fighting someone.

❦

I headed to my bedroom, sweaty and pleasantly exhausted after my lesson with Lamord. The fencing master was more skilled than Hamlet, and I intended to make the most of his tutelage while I could. I'd return to Denmark predatory. Let the prince try to beat me. My skill would place me on more equal footing again, and maybe we could return to our friendship after all.

In the living room, I passed Henri eyeing the brick wall as if it would reveal more empty spaces for the new sketch he held loosely in one hand.

The air felt cool outside, so I immediately grabbed Cicero and headed out onto the roof. My window opened to a sloping pitch invisible to the street below. Dusk fell lightly over the city. The sounds of shoppers below muted as though in adoration of the coming night when new promises bloomed in Paris. It became its namesake, its gorgeous shadow self, the City of Lights.

I propped myself up and began to read. Immediately, I wished I'd brought my Latin dictionary with me. Cicero's sentences meandered, and words could click into several places given their endings. Each choice changed the outcome. But I'd had enough practice that I could basically understand his argument, albeit with white fuzz gracing the edges of my thought. I needed something to focus on besides the future awaiting Ophelia and Hamlet and me, and this artificial handicap simply made my complete focus necessary.

Virtue, he said, had three cooperating branches: Wisdom, Temperance, and Justice. The second was not my forte. I wrote a question in the margin about limits of vengeance in accordance with justice, when a creak sounded behind me.

I twisted.

"Hold on," said Julien, half out of the window already. "I hear piano. I'm not ready for another concert." He disappeared.

Moments later, the music stopped and he returned with Henri in tow.

The three of us lounged there until it was too dark to read, then one by one stowed our books.

I put my hands behind my head and stared up. "What was she like, the girl?" I asked Henri.

"She was a dream. You would have liked her."

"Too much, probably," Julien piped in. "But who needs women when you're Damon and Pythias? Have you gotten that far?"

"There are three of us," I pointed out. "I know the story." I hadn't read far enough in Cicero to encounter his version yet.

Legends talked about Pythias committing treason against the king and being sentenced to death. In the story, Pythias asks to set his affairs in order before he dies, but he is only allowed to go if a friend stands as surety to die in his place if he doesn't return. Damon, his friend with whom he shares everything, offers without hesitation. Pythias is late returning, so Damon prepares to die. Then, at the last moment, Pythias returns. Rumors suggest he was held captive by pirates on the way back and had to fight his way home—at least that was the version I liked best. The king, moved by their friendship, commutes the sentence and asks to join their circle of unbreakable trust. Even when the friends say no, he still lets them go.

"Perhaps you're the king, hm?" Henri said, looking at Julien before smiling at me.

Julien cursed and shoved him. "I'm Pythias, and you two are my Damons."

"Then now's the time to commit treason," Henri said mildly.

I released one hand to fiddle with the pages of the book where it lay at my side. There was always some truth in stories, whether they spoke of ghosts and monsters or kings and queens.

"*Pythias* is a corruption, you know. It should be *Phintias*." Julien's tone switched from dock worker to professor in an instant.

"I'll never say *Phintias*," I replied. My mother told me the story of Damon and Pythias when I was a tiny child. *When you find loyal friends, hold them close to your soul*, she said. I had.

A breeze swept over us. Fingers of chill ran across my body. Summer was ending and nothing could stop the march of time from depositing us, relentlessly, into a future when we'd be scattered.

I tried to picture it, but only managed to conjure images from the past: riding together through Paris streets, sitting in church with my mother, talking as Ophelia arranged flowers, walking the Seine in search of a good time, drinking with Hamlet... I couldn't imagine myself living in the chancellery of Kronborg Castle with a meek wife and small children, beholden to the desires of my father and the royal family. I wanted to make them proud, but I didn't want to be near them. Staying in Paris was all but forbidden, though. I could dally for a year, maybe two, but then I'd have to go back, leaving so much that I loved behind.

This city, these people, were my *raison d'être*.

I sighed. "What are we going to *do* after this? Why did we study Classics?"

"Because we are not small men," Julien said, angling up. Faint light filtering up from the street bathed his face. His expression burned. "Greek and Latin are gateways to culture and history and literature and philosophy, not small talk and commerce."

He always was more an ancient Roman than a Dane. I smiled. "Yes, but you're still going to work for your father."

He flopped down, mouth twisted in a sardonic grimace. "Of course I am. *Labor vincit omnia.*" After a pause, he added, "I'll find some poor bastard to take my place. Maybe a few years."

I knew enough of Julien's brothers to know that they could never take over the family business. News of their factory reached even Kronborg, largely because Julien's father was so vocal in politics. The castle watched the family warily.

"And you, Henri?" I asked.

"I don't know." His soft voice had steel in it. For all his artistic introversion, Henri could be the most intense among us. He sopped up life like a sponge, greedy for feeling, for truth, for sensation.

His family, too, was wealthy, but I knew he didn't like taking money from his relatives. The Battlements was the only exception. No one complained about that.

I in the center between my two halves, we lay in silence for a while on the shore of an unknown future.

***

The sun warmed me and the breeze chilled me. Even then, at seven, I was all things at once.

I remember Ophelia splashing in the waves of the Sound, wetting the hem of her sky-blue gown. Father wouldn't have approved. Violets adorned her hair messily, as though she were a creature that belonged to the element of woods and water.

I walked alongside Mother, racing ahead then turning back to hold her hand. Sand gritted somewhere in my shoes. Mother was like a painting. In my memory, she's always a perfect watercolor, skirt caught demurely in the breeze, loose blonde tendrils framing her face. Or she is like a Roman statue—that straight nose and fair skin sloping up to cheekbones I inherited but didn't wear as well. Her far-seeing gaze mirrored art too, at once present with an animal awareness and fraught with thought. I've often wondered if I should have known then by the seriousness of her eyes. I spent too much time looking for crabs and scanning for ships and splashing sea water on Ophelia to notice.

A hand gripped my upper arm. "Oh!" Mother cried.

I looked up. Her attention was riveted some distance ahead.

A large white bird squatted there. Its beak jutted grotesquely forward, skin hanging from it as though it could inflate like a balloon.

"A pelican," Mother explained. The smell of her rosemary perfume wafted on the breeze. "Ophelia! Come here and look."

Reluctantly, Ophelia padded up the sand to stand by Mother's elbow with me.

"Pelicans are nature's greatest mothers. When there is no food to feed their young, they will rip themselves open and offer their very blood to drink. There's no greater sacrifice. They remind us of Christ." She sighed. Maybe it was regretful. "A pelican. I've never seen one here before, so enjoy this moment. She might never come again."

The most painful part of the memory comes next.

I ran at the bird, whooping and waving my arms. Mother might have yelled to stop me. Either way, the pelican scuttled sideways, snapped its huge beak, and spread improbably wide wings to fly.

Ophelia laughed and so did I. Mother didn't.

I should have known.

❧

Three days later, Ophelia's letter finally came. I ripped the top of the paper getting the envelope open. She was all right! I don't know why I doubted it. I don't know why I catastrophized to the utmost any time my mind had free play. But my fears weren't all allayed. Why had it taken so long? Was there trouble, a secret? Something with Hamlet?

I blew out a breath and sat at the sideboard I used for a desk, where I'd bought a vase of hothouse roses that reminded me of her. They towered, blood-red and blooming, above the pen stand and bottle of ink.

At the top of the paper, in the corner, Ophelia had drawn a miniature rose. When we were teenagers, I called her "rose of May" once and the nickname had stuck. I forget why I'd said it in the first place. I could have been teasing, but I kept my teasing gentle where she was concerned, as though she might break under anything stronger than a light rebuke.

Henri cast me a glance from where he sat behind me playing the piano. I think it was Debussy.

My dear brother,

I trust you made it safely to Paris. You ought to write Father to confirm it, since he worries about you.

Life here continues as it always does. Between sewing and tending my little garden, I soak up the good weather by walking in the courtyard or down to the beach with friends. I have been helping the Queen more often. She requests me particularly, which softens the news that I feel compelled to share with you. It shouldn't come as something undesirable, as the Queen herself would sanction what has begun.

I have been reticent to write, knowing your tendency toward strong reactions. I pray you rein in your judgment and remind yourself that you've expressed trust in me. I've always confided in you. This time should be no different. Take my gesture as a continued sign of faith and love for you. I hope I should merit such honesty from you as well.

Lord Hamlet has expressed an interest in spending private time with me. We exchange letters almost daily and he told me he plans to continue courting me from Wittenberg. I think he truly likes me. We enjoy each other's company and he treats me as a gentleman should. The most difficult part to believe is that the prince would choose me for his companion.

We have not left the palace together, but the society magazines haunt him so closely that it's possible there could be an entry about the two of us soon, and I wanted you to hear the truth from me before you encountered it at the news-stand. How dreadful would it be if you felt I had hidden the truth from you! I assure you that his intentions appear honorable. He says he is enamored with me. (I am almost embarrassed to write the word.)

I hope you can forgive him for exaggerating stories about you. All have sinned, as Paul writes, and I know I am no exception either. I love you both and want to see you reconciled.

I wait eagerly for your return at Christmas. The castle always feels lonelier without you.

Ever yours,

Ophelia

I stared at the letter. Hamlet and Ophelia. My suspicions were correct. They exchanged letters every day. I couldn't help but be jealous.

My blood felt hot, so I unbuttoned the collar of my shirt. Was this revenge, as I had thought, or did Hamlet truly like Ophelia more than the others who received his flirtations? Ophelia was intelligent, but Hamlet had an aura about him of power and eloquence and beauty. You must understand, once Hamlet's attention turned fully to you, it was difficult not to hope it would last. I gulped in breath, trying to process what I had learned.

Perhaps... perhaps, she could benefit him with her innocence and he could elevate her with his power. Perhaps he wouldn't hurt her.

A mad part of me wanted to believe her and think the best of Hamlet. Another part wanted to crash my fist into his face. I was blowing apart like the crest of a wave in a storm.

It was an honor.

It was a travesty.

Love for my sister was the only rock in the tempest.

Grinding my teeth, I slid out a sheet of paper to reply. The pen poised at the ready, but then returned to its stand. I had to rid my body of this intolerable tension. Not knowing what I planned to do, I went out.

3

OCTOBER

O ctober came in a storm of rain and leaves and darkness. Magic laced the air of The Battlements and the university, as though our readings were incantations rather than the musings of old teachers.

I heard more often from Ophelia now that her secret was out. Rapidly, she was becoming a favorite of Queen Gertrude. Ophelia defended the Queen's reputation as stringently as she defended Hamlet's. Her belief in them read as innocent piety more than willful blindness, but how deep was the line between those two? Perhaps she was right about them. Hamlet could love Ophelia—she insisted on it more intensely now, which twisted my stomach—and the Queen probably was faithful to the King. I'd known them my entire life, and the King was nothing but kind to his wife.

Cicero became *Satires* by Horace followed by the French *Le Roman de la Rose*. Drafting papers reminded me of the class on diplomatic writing Hamlet hated so much. I could lose myself in the words of others, but I wasn't good with them myself. Even Hamlet's mocking version of a professional letter read better than mine when I put in full effort. I preferred to go out into the city, trailing Henri to the Gustave Moreau or, better, finding entertainment on tennis courts or in taverns. I could quiet my thoughts and lose myself in myriad ways, in the pleasure of drink or soft company. Away from Kronborg, I wasn't important enough to notice, even when my distractions turned to wildness.

❧

The three of us sat in a row on the ground in front of a painting depicting Hesiod and the Muses. Artwork crammed the walls of the dim space. A magnificently sinuous staircase wound through the middle of the room like a dancer.

Henri sketched a copy of the picture with a soft pencil, his strokes sure. Julien and I might as well not have been there, he focused so intently. In Julien, however, I could feel some of my own restlessness as we watched Henri work.

I finished the last of the baguette and cheese I'd brought with me and stood. The museum would close soon. "We'll meet you at home," I said. Julien silently joined me as I went out.

Night blanketed the city. Wind cut through the streets, driving sheets of rain diagonally across our faces as we found our bicycles. Wet leaves plastered against our woolen coats. I gripped the cold handlebars and swung myself up. Water splashed beneath the tires as we rode, scattering reflected light in the black pools of the street. Drops fell from the brim of Julien's hat whenever I caught sight of him. Chilly rainwater crept down my back and ran down my temples.

By the time we reached The Battlements, I couldn't wait to strip off my clothes and change into dry ones.

"Night for goblins," Julien declared as we crossed the threshold, tracking in water but careful not to let it corrupt the books. We touched the skull.

An unfinished essay sat in the typewriter but I didn't have the energy to work on it.

Minutes later, toweled off and in striped nightclothes, I emerged into the main room again. Julien had removed his ever-present cap. It hung on the window lever to dry. His dark hair stuck up crazily as if he had rubbed it with a cloth as I had with mine. I had the stupid thought that his forehead was bigger than I remembered.

Henri hadn't yet arrived, but it was typical of him to stay until the night guard found him and ordered him to leave. Sometimes they didn't find him. The Gustave Moreau was smaller and less crowded than the Louvre, which was just as close to our flat. The Moreau felt like ours more than the larger museum did.

I boiled some water and made toddies for us to warm up. I handed Julien the hot mug and he stretched out his legs comfortably. Rain lashed against the windows.

"This reminds me of the night my cousin disappeared," he said.

"What happened?" Hopefully Julien wouldn't indulge his penchant for ghost stories. He knew a disconcerting number of them and they affected me more than I was willing to admit, for a variety of reasons, but I was no child, so I leaned back in my chair, raising my eyebrows as though daring him to go on.

"A month before, he started having dreams that would wake him every night screaming. It was always the same dream, about a creature dripping down from a tree—those were his words—huge and black, with clawed hands and long fingers. Its mouth was invisible until it opened, and then it seemed to rip the beast into two halves of rowed teeth."

"Rowed teeth?"

"Shut up. It was terrifying, and my cousin felt like it was stalking him. He started to sense it even in the daytime. He'd see it out of the corner of his eye in shadows, or in smoke, and especially on nights like this." He took a sip, apparently enjoying the story.

My insides unclenched a little. This couldn't be true, then. Some of his stories were.

"A week before, he started seeing handprints outside his window. His mother cleaned them off, but it happened again, this time on the inside of the pane, in oil. The handprint wouldn't come off. Then finally, when he woke up screaming the next time, he had claw marks on his neck. A storm came." He nodded toward the window. "And he vowed he'd never sleep again. The hours ticked by. Tick, tick, tick."

Julien leaned forward on his knees and set his drink on the lid of the trunk.

My heart thumped in my chest despite myself.

"Tick, tick... The floors and windows creaked, almost driving him mad wondering if it was the storm or some nightmare creature crawling out of the dark to get him. Then, right by his ear, a *squeeeeeeak* as fingers dragged down the mirror he had propped by the bed. He might as well have been a block of ice, but he slowly turned around to look. The thing clung to the inside of the mirror like a spider. The inside, where his reflection was supposed to be."

Julien sat back abruptly and I released a breath.

"That's the last time anyone heard of him alive. A night just like this one. Four days later they found his body, mutilated, hanging from a tree."

The toddy turned to bile in my throat.

The outside door crashed open. I jumped so fiercely my drink spilled. Raucous laughter burst from Julien as Henri barged into the room.

"What's so funny?" Henri asked.

"Nothing," I said.

"Our Laertes is afraid of goblins and fairies and witches." Julien rose, knocking back the rest of his drink.

"No, I'm not." My hands balled into fists.

"I scared the shit out of you with that story."

"No, you didn't."

Henri looked like he was still shedding the artistic imagination that had consumed him in the museum. "I'm sure it was frightening," he murmured, ever the peacekeeper.

He immediately went to dry off and Julien drifted to his room soon after, leaving me alone.

My blood still pulsed with the aftermath of the story, though I hated to admit it. No doubt there would be more stories like that one, with All Hallows' Eve coming in just a few weeks, a time, Julien reminded me, when the living and dead mingled. I had to steel myself, but something about those stories crept under my skin, uncomfortable as a needle. I couldn't simply shake them off. Maybe because I believed in the supernatural. In church, pastors always spoke of demons, or seraphim, or Nephilim.

Leftover madeleines sat in a paper bag on the counter. I took them out one by one and ate them, waiting for the frightful sensation to pass. Instead, it grew. The flaky cookies became chalk on my tongue and I stopped eating.

A book? Perhaps I could read, nothing so challenging as Latin, but a novel. Yes, that could work. Or I could look outside to assure myself nothing was lurking.

I headed toward the door, breaths shallow, my fingertips growing numb with dread. I reached out and touched the knob. It felt wet-cold. I let my fingers slide off.

She was here.

Waves of storm hit the walls, the door, the windows, masking any other sound. But she didn't come loudly. She was always silent.

The room smelled suddenly of rosemary.

If I had looked down at my chest, I'm sure I would have seen my nightshirt tremble with the force of my beating heart. I turned back toward the living room.

A female figure stood in the room, pale as death, with dark, vacant eyes fixed on mine. She also wore a nightdress. I remembered it well.

My mouth dried. I couldn't swallow or make a sound. I felt as if I were choking.

Her body was slack, lifeless, except for the eyes that glared. She seemed to float just above the ground, high enough that she had to angle her head down to look at me.

I fought the urge to cringe away.

She blinked, and the eyes were my mother's, and then she was gone.

⁂

The next day found me crammed into a corner of the Sainte-Geneviève Library beside a bust of Nero, looking up books on the spirit world. The occult section of the library wasn't the most popular, and that suited my mood perfectly. I wanted to be alone.

Light streamed in through the high windows down into the main room. Long tables lay in neat horizontal rows on the floor below me. That large space for study felt too exposed. I needed secrecy, privacy, in order to banish spirits.

My mother's appearance the night before wasn't the first. I sometimes smelled rosemary when I walked alone down deserted streets or felt eyes on me as I studied on the roof. My peripheral vision would catch a dark figure—sometimes loving but more often accusing—that would vanish when I moved my head.

This couldn't go on. What *this* was, I barely could have said, but a few solitary hours drowning in books had to help. At least it could ameliorate the sense of shame that pervaded my senses and replace a useless apology with something more concrete.

I'm sorry. I'm sorry.

Nero sneered at me. I picked up *Phenomena of Spiritualism* and flicked through the chapter index. Was there anything about preventing hauntings?

Not by destroying a ghost, I assured myself, as though that were possible. *Only, moving it to another, better realm.*

I hardly knew what I was talking about. I just knew these apparitions had to stop. The most common old advice was to complete some action that could ease the spirit's passing, but I knew the time for that had long passed.

After several hours, I found nothing more than a folk remedy tucked into a medieval pamphlet. Luc carried the herbs I needed in his shop, so I bought some when I returned home.

I smoked two cigarettes on the fire escape landing before writing Ophelia. Her latest letter excerpted a song that Hamlet had written for her—grammatically insensible but mouthwatering as chocolate ganache. She provided it as proof of his sincerity after I'd cast doubt on the subject of their budding relationship.

I still felt doubt, and guilt, and confusion, and all the emotions in my body I'd sooner die than endure much longer.

The rest of the school year. Then... Then what?

I attacked my new composition to Ophelia with enough force to rip through the paper. I mended the hole sloppily with wax. It would certainly crack before it got to Denmark. But now the letter had character.

"You have character," my mother said once. "Make sure you have both kinds, the unique and the good." Superimposed over the memory was my last view of her unseeing face. I shuddered.

What was wrong with me? Words wouldn't come. All I'd written was *My dear Ophelia.* My heart fairly burst with thoughts for her but none verbalized themselves, certainly not as Hamlet had done with his poem or song or whatever it was. I loved her more than Hamlet ever could. I was sure of it, yet I had no words at all.

I couldn't tell her about my life, about my suspicions. She'd think I was mad. Perhaps I was. Was this what happened to Mother before...?

I blinked and dug into my pocket for the sage I'd purchased. Inhaling its scent, I gave up on the letter for now. I'd try ridding the house of ghosts before Henri or Julien came home, then I could evaluate what to say to my sister.

My mother lay sprawled across her bed in a white nightgown, like a woman swooning in a painting. One arm was flung over her head and the other clutched the hem of her neckline. Blankets bunched around her legs as though she'd thrashed them off.

When I crept in to tell her of my nightmare, I thought she was asleep, but something in her pose made me stop. For a while, I couldn't figure out what it was. The theatricality? The stillness? At seven, I was even less attuned to nuance. It was her open eyes, glassy, like marbles.

I shifted my weight, and the gaze didn't shift with me. "Mother?" My voice was a whisper.

It was a strangely intimate moment when no one else knew.

My beautiful mother in bed, dead, and I, alive. The juxtaposition was like a conversation so profound it twisted the air itself, the room, and my stomach. We existed in some in-between place where everyone's breath held. As long as I didn't move, it wasn't real. I could still do something to save her and prevent tragedy.

Oddly, whenever I looked back on that moment, one prevailing impression was of shame. Mother never would have wanted me to see her that way, and yet I stood there, violating what were surely her last wishes.

I didn't leave. I didn't move. I should have tried to revive her. At least the useless gesture would have been one of love.

That's how Father found me, frozen, utterly unable to move. When he gasped and touched my shoulder to usher me out of the room, I flung myself on the floor and screamed. I'd never cried so hard in my life.

Father finally dragged me out. "Compose yourself!" he hissed. His whole face shone red with unshed tears. "A man doesn't cry." His lip trembled afterward and his body shuddered with the effort to keep from weeping.

I couldn't stop. Someone came and took me to my room. I wanted to stay and find some sense in what had happened. I wanted to be a good boy and change her mind. I wanted to stay by her side like some fairy tale prince until she came back to life. Once she was taken away, I knew we would never speak of her again, and I couldn't bear it. Even then, I couldn't bear it.

⚜

Luc's chemist shop looked particularly dreamlike in the witching time of night. It was lonely and empty, as it often was when I passed it on the way home. All Hallows' Eve was approaching, and Luc had the look of a creature sworn to hunt children and feed them his potions.

The fanciful comparison lifted my spirits a little. They had been low for weeks. Between difficult translations and mixing sage with running water, I couldn't see the sky from the hole where I dwelt. Even Henri and Julien couldn't always reach me in my black moods.

Ophelia, my best connection to Kronborg, spoke rapturously of being able to see Hamlet in person this month during his break from university. My blood curdled at the thought, though I chided myself.

Ophelia said I held grudges. I did. I tried not to, but I did.

My grudge had shifted away from his accusations about me to simply who he was as a man. I should have been as self-possessed, as brilliant, as eloquent. Where his conversation sparkled, I repeated myself. Hamlet was my foil, showing off my ineptitude, growing paranoia, recklessness, and lack of direction.

Already the charm of my romantic notion about the chemist had worn off by the time I climbed to The Battlements. My breath frosted the air in front of my face as I topped the fire escape and opened the door.

In the living room, amid the clutter, stood three figures.

I stopped.

One was a woman, a woman in trousers. It was a woman, though, with two perfect Fibonacci spirals of dark hair at her temples. She stood beside Henri. She looked tall and tough. The brown trousers reached to her slim waist and could have kept going. She was slim all the way up, almost like a man. Her loose white dress shirt tied in a bow at the side of her neck. Her eyes were as dark and intense as the actress Asta Nielsen's.

"Ah, here he is," said Henri, gesturing toward me.

I hadn't noticed how messy the room was before now. It felt crowded with four people in it. The coffee table chest had been shoved under the wide piano bench to make room.

"Josephine, this is Laertes. Laertes, meet Josephine."

She held out a hand. I took it. Her skin was soft but her shake felt firm.

"Laertes, like the father of Odysseus?" she asked with a smile. None of the lisping affectation of the Danish court reached her voice. Instead, her French voice was rich and rasping. I'd never met a creature like this. She didn't fit into the neat categories I understood. I didn't know if I liked that.

"Yes, that's how my father discovered the name."

"Henri found her at the Louvre," Julien explained as Henri put his hand round her waist.

"His sketches are beguiling," she said. "They mirror nature perfectly."

I searched the wall for a new addition. I didn't notice one, though I couldn't help realizing how many of his pieces depicted the nude marble torsos of men and women with all their curves and musculature.

"I guess they do," I agreed, distracted.

Josephine had broken into our sanctum, a feat no other woman had been able to accomplish. All our rendezvous had taken place elsewhere. The Battlements were sacred. Curiosity outweighed my irritation, though, as Henri ushered her to take a seat in his chair.

"Are you... who are you?" I asked again, unable to look away from her outfit for long. Was that a costume, or did she want to be mistaken for a man on the street?

She laughed, throaty and sweet. "Josephine Roche."

"Stop staring," said Julien. "He stares."

"I do not stare."

"You're doing it now."

I couldn't deny that, but I looked away.

"Everyone stares," she declared, carelessly knocking a cigarette into her hand. Simply because of the size of The Battlements, the three of us rarely smoked inside, preferring the balcony or roof. "When you do something different, everyone does."

Henri gave her a light. She breathed in and looked around appraisingly before letting out the smoke. With a genteel smile, she returned her attention to Henri. "That was how I found you." She didn't elaborate, but pulled out the cigarette to give him a bold kiss on the cheek.

After a few seconds, Julien caught my eye. I had been staring again.

Dear Ophelia,

Women in Paris are different than in Denmark. They speak their minds more freely and some even wear trousers. It seems unnatural to me, as though they would be men themselves. Would you ever wear trousers? I know Father would hate it but I can't help wondering.

My dear brother,

Father sends his regards. I don't think I'd ever wear trousers, especially since he would disapprove, but whyever would it be unnatural? Women have two legs, as men have. Too many men think our value lies solely in beauty, but it lies in honesty too, in a beautiful mind. In that, we're not so different. These women sound interesting. Where did you meet them?

"Stop leaning forward!" Lamord barked. His taut frame looked dangerous with irritation.

I corrected my stance.

A few flicks and parries later, he got another touch and stepped back, tearing off his helmet. "Distance, distance!" he cried. "It must be exact. You must know your body's parameters and parry with the air, not only your blade. This separates mediocrity from greatness." His eyes burned like a drunkard's, set deep in a face that was all skin and cheekbones, like an anatomical study. Tight brown curls sat crisply atop his head. The wax whorling his mustache had gotten smudged in the helmet. He seemed to sense the asymmetry; he removed one glove, smoothed his lip, and replaced the glove.

"I'm trying."

"Try harder."

I asked for this, I reminded myself. If I were ever to beat Hamlet and have a skill that even the prince couldn't master as well, it was fencing. But today's failures in class blurred my movements and made me reckless. I needed more finesse, and all I had was more aggression.

"One more, eh?" Lamord said, replacing his mask.

Lean back, I reminded myself.

The master goaded me forward with each flick of his wrist. Sweat coated my face. I knew I held my shoulders too rigidly, but I was determined to get the move right this time. His attack had to be coming soon. I would lean back and...

Thwack!

"Too slow," Lamord declared. "Of course too slow. You had no plasticity. A fencer must be lithe and graceful. It is cunning, not brute force, that wins."

My nostrils flared in frustration. Never enough. I was all potential and nothing actual. My chest heaved.

"Eh." Lamord tapped my uniform lightly with his foil. His body language softened. "I must be cruel only to be kind."

I grunted in response, packing up my things to go. I knew better than to ask him to extend the lesson. Lamord lived on a tight schedule. He was a competitive fencer himself, taught lessons, and owned horses that he rode in exhibitions several times a month.

Hauling my gear outside, I mounted my green bicycle and set off down the avenue toward home. I would have gone faster, if not for my bulky pack.

It was probably because I rode so slowly that I saw the magazine. Proudly displayed at a newsstand, a society paper shouted the headline: THE HEARTTHROB PRINCE, IN LOVE? Above the headline was a stylized version of a popular photograph of Hamlet, adjusted to look as if he were gazing after a hazy woman in the distance.

I jerked the bicycle to a halt and dumped the fencing gear on the ground to get a better look. The first pages of the magazine were all ads for cars, cigarettes, appliances. Where was the damn article?

Finally, there it was. "Lovestruck Prince of Denmark Spotted with New Sweetheart."

"Oh my god," I mouthed.

On October 17, our intrepid reporters caught a glimpse of Prince Hamlet of Denmark, age 21, engaged in activities that are sure to trouble much of the single female populace of Europe. I wish the prince all the best in his endeavors and by no means intend by this article to criticize his actions. Whatever the charismatic heir was doing, it certainly appeared that he was taking advantage of the gay weather that day to entertain a new lady. Yes, that's right. He was seen in the company of a charming young woman of little fortune or stature, the beautiful Ophelia Belleforest, age 18. Our sources have discovered that she is the daughter of the Danish King's advisor. Could this be a secret romance from childhood as they played in the palace together? Cont. on pg. 19.

Someone snorted close to my ear. "Another money-grubbing whore, no doubt," a man's gruff voice declared. "Do they have to tell us about every—"

I dropped the magazine and smashed him in the jaw. My knuckles stung from the impact and I saw through the haze of my rage that he was older than I'd thought. Maybe in his fifties.

He tried scrambling to his feet. Blood leaked into his mustache. I wouldn't let him up. He gritted his teeth and kicked his legs wildly, like a caged animal might. I punched him again.

People screamed around us, the newsstand suddenly a flurry of activity. I didn't know exactly what was happening.

He gripped my upper arms with a stronger hold than I would have guessed by looking at the man. Paper crinkled as we scuffled over the fallen magazine. He landed a couple hits to my face but I had the upper hand.

"Stop! That's enough!" Rough hands hauled me back. I couldn't find my feet and fell on my behind, still glaring through my knees at the other man who'd called Ophelia a whore.

A different policeman than the one who'd ripped me away helped the man to his feet.

I spit.

"Hey!" someone exclaimed.

I glowered, but the adrenaline was wearing off. The white, square shape of the magazine in the dirt caught my eye once more. I raised my hands for the policemen's benefit and slowly stooped to pick it up. The cover had torn, but I hadn't read page 19.

"No public disturbance!"

I was shoved away from the man, who looked ready to murder me.

Gathering my things, I once more pedaled away, breathing hard. Something warm and salty slid into my mouth. My nose was bleeding as the man's had been.

By the time I approached The Battlements, strangers got out of my way. I clambered up the fire escape with the gracefulness of an angry rhinoceros.

Inside, I found Henri and Josephine both reading. He sat on the floor and she lay with her head in his lap, one knee propped up.

"Falling out at tennis?" Julien guessed from where he sat in his habitual armchair.

Josephine lowered the book above her head and gasped, sitting up. Her movement caused Henri to look up too.

I struggled for a moment with my bag full of unwieldy fencing uniform and foil before I disentangled myself and threw the magazine at Julien's feet.

He raised his eyebrows to the brim of his cap.

Henri leaned over and read the headline. "Is this about Ophelia?" he asked, casting me a concerned look.

"Even if it is, it doesn't explain the black eye," Julien quipped.

I dropped my head, muttering. "Doesn't matter."

"Who's Ophelia?" Josephine asked, fishing for a bookmark.

"His sister," Henri explained.

"Does Prince Hamlet fancy her? That's not bad, right?" She jostled forward for a better look.

"It's... complicated," Henri said.

I scooped up the paper and proceeded to my own room, where I could be alone. The rest of the article merely speculated on the nature of the relationship, inferring much more than an innocent walk should have insinuated. The article served as a stark reminder that Hamlet's break from Wittenberg gave them more time to be alone together, and I feared this article would make its way into my father's hands somehow. He always wanted to know what was going on. I doubted he would approve of this flirtation.

A knock sounded at my door. Still huffy, I answered. All three of them crowded the doorway. The sight irritated me at first, but then I felt oddly touched. A raw piece of meat, thinner than a steak, dangled from Julien's hand.

Josephine was the first to rush forward. "Come on," she said. "You've had a bad day."

I didn't realize until I moved into the living room that Henri held the bottle of absinthe we kept stocked in the kitchen. Josephine took out little glasses as I positioned the meat on my swelling eye. None of them asked more questions. Julien and Henri could no doubt infer a number of likely scenarios, given my history of fighting, but Josephine could have no idea why I'd returned bloody and bruised, yet she kept refilling my glass of absinthe until the edges of the room blurred into laughter.

❦ 4 ❦
NOVEMBER

Only three weeks after playing Blindman's Bluff, I sat with Hamlet in the tunnels below the castle, where light looked medieval and I could picture treasure buried beneath the floor.

The points of the metal jacks dug into my palms as I grabbed them to the beat of the bouncing ball.

Hamlet had only picked up seven before he lost the beat.

I held seven now.

"Beetle-faced clown," he said as the ball rose and I scooped up another jack. His eyes followed my hand.

The points slipped, then held. I grabbed tight and the jacks didn't fall. I won!

I laughed and squeezed my handful of treasure. Hamlet picked up the last remaining jack and tossed it at me. When I opened my hand again, blood coated two of the metal points where they'd pierced the skin.

My laughter faltered. What right had I to laugh, to be happy at all? Punishment was more fitting. Mother had died only a week ago. I should be buried in a cave, never to see loved ones again. I should be haunted by her disappointed ghost. I should...

I swiped at new tears, dropping the jacks. I was blind again, but this time I couldn't take off a blindfold and see the sun. It wouldn't shine for me.

Arms surrounded me and, surly, I tried to shake them off. They tightened and Hamlet kissed the top of my head. I'd seen his mother do the same thing to him a thousand times.

I sniffed, finally allowing him to hug me.

As soon as I relaxed into him, Hamlet shoved me away. "Now stop being a sissy and watch me get nine." His mouth was set, jaw thrust forward, all concentration on the game. His gaze didn't lift to mine, as though his focus could direct my attention too and lead me away from my loss. It was unconventional charity.

I smeared the blood in my palm, took a sharp, steadying breath. "You won't do it," I managed.

"I'm a prince," he replied, his attention flicking back to me for just a second. "I'll make you say I got nine. Just wait."

"What are you reading?" I asked Josephine one night.

She sat on the piano bench, long legs crossed in front of her as she faced the room, smoking with one hand and reading with the other. Her trousers were gray that day, and she wore a mauve silk headdress. Light from the candle atop the piano cast glinting waves across the silk. Julien and Henri were out.

Josephine shifted so her elbows rested on the fallboard. "You've never heard of Elizabeth Barrett Browning?"

I frowned. "No. A woman author?"

"*The* woman author," she said. "I hear England nearly chose her for their Poet Laureate. You're very old-fashioned, aren't you?"

She regarded me not unkindly, but as though I were an interesting specimen. Or maybe just as though I were interesting.

"Well, I don't know that I'd say that," I hedged, feeling criticism behind the term. My question had been stupid in retrospect. Of course *Elizabeth* was a woman.

Suddenly, I wondered very much how she came to be *not* old-fashioned. How did one make their way in the world without a guide to light the way? I looked again at her trousers. They were growing on me.

"What's the book about?" I gestured to the copy she held.

Before answering, Josephine took a drag on her cigarette and let out a stream of smoke. "It's about a woman named Aurora Leigh. She's a poet. It recounts the story of her life, discovering her talents after she loses her father."

"Oh," I said. It didn't sound thrilling to me, but perhaps that was hypocritical. After all, I liked Livy. "That sounds fascinating."

She gave me a knowing smile. Had I sounded sarcastic? I hadn't meant to.

"It is," she confirmed.

"Then I want to read it." I felt surer by the second.

"Do you?"

"Yes."

She handed it to me. The book was thick, with a burnt orange cover etched with a riotous pattern of pansies. In elegant script, it read "Aurora Leigh by Mrs. Browning." The pages felt soft with use.

"You know," said Josephine, putting out her cigarette in the ash tray, "no one else has asked me about it."

I felt an odd surge of pride at that. "We have a lot to read for university," I replied dismissively.

She tapped my foot with hers and laughed. Though Josephine practically lived at The Battlements these days, this was the first time the two of us had been alone, I realized. I cleared my throat.

"Why don't you read to me then?"

"What?"

"Your university reading."

That sounded too intimate for... whatever we were. Probably friends, although she still confused me more than a bottle of wine could do. "I don't—"

"You can get your work done and cure my boredom at once. Doesn't that sound grand?" Mischief glimmered in her darkly lined eyes. She reminded me of Hamlet then, a mind so active that boredom settled like a butterfly any time there was little stimulation.

"Why do you wear trousers?" I blurted.

Her guffaw was decidedly unladylike. She tamed her laugh and gave a graceful little hem at the end.

My face heated. Perhaps I was prying, as my father was wont to do, but I carried on. "I... I think it's a fair and open question."

"Because I want to. Don't you like them?" She lifted one long leg, toe pointed. I had to lean back—I'd been leaning forward—to avoid her. Her foot rose to my chin and back down.

"I... don't... Yes. I don't know."

She smirked. No shame at all, as I would have felt in her place.

"When did you first wear them?" I asked.

"Oh..." She waved her hand. "Ages ago."

She couldn't have been older than twenty.

She must have seen my incredulous expression because she sighed and continued, "A friend invited me to a private club a few years ago. Don't ask me what it was called. I doubt it had a name. Most of the women there wore trousers and short hair. I thought they seemed... free." She gave a small elegant shrug.

Free? Free from what?

She kicked me again. "Now for that story."

"Are you sure?" I asked, burning to know more about the club. "It's in Latin."

"I adore a man who speaks several languages."

I blushed but couldn't fathom why.

That was how Julien and Henri found us later, sitting across from one another as I read to her from Catullus.

I faltered mid-sentence as Henri entered. Josephine leapt up and kissed him on the cheek.

"Have you been here with only Laertes for company?" Julien exclaimed, tugging off his overcoat and touching the skull. "I feel bad for you."

"He's not bad company," she said lightly.

I rose and tucked *Aurora Leigh* under Catullus before ducking into my room and throwing them both on the bed. I rejoined the others in time to hear Henri ask, "Do you want to go out, *mon coeur?*"

"It's too cold for that. You want to stay in, don't you?" Julien said.

Josephine tugged on the sleeve of Henri's brown sweater. "We can show them what we've been practicing."

"You devil," I said to Henri. "What have you been practicing?"

"It was her idea," Henri said, smiling at her.

They looked striking together, like living art, all dark eyes and graceful lines. They didn't tell their secret.

Instead, we set to work discovering what food we had for supper. There was nothing for a sumptuous meal, but, since Josephine had all but stayed with us the past few weeks, we had no one but ourselves to impress. Together, we found two crusty baguettes, *rillettes de porc*, cornichons, apples, clementines, a small wheel of brie, apricot preserves, and several hard boiled eggs. Dishes clinked among cups of coffee or gin. It wasn't late, but November skies in Paris were always gloomy and dark. Night settled early.

After dinner, we ate soaked lady fingers and sucked the honey from our fingers. The skull gazed pleasantly at us from his shelf. I must have looked rakish then, completely unfit for polite society. The idea filled me with savage glee. Honey coated my lips, and breadcrumbs littered the floor. We draped ourselves across the floor and furniture with no sense of decorum, but only comfort or impulse.

There was no ghost to haunt this candlelit room, there were no expectations of me to meet my father's grand hopes, there was no gnawing concern about Ophelia. My chest ached with the fleetingness of the night, and I thought I could happily die.

Piano chords in halting groups of three sounded above me like the flourish signaling the beginning of a cabaret. Henri roosted in his usual spot. Josephine stood with one hand on his shoulder. Perhaps this is what they'd been practicing. I sat up to see better, leaning against the bottom of an armchair, and cast a look at Julien. He shrugged one big shoulder, eyes sparkling.

Josephine began singing. The song was familiar, but I couldn't place it. My knowledge of English was limited, but I'd heard these lyrics before. "*With me*," she sang, "*it's what to be. Now make me some suggestions.*"

Julien caught on before I did. He joined in, his brusque voice joining hers. "*When you're after fun and laughter, this aggravates you.*"

Josephine slid over to us, stealing Julien's cap from him. I had tried that in jest several years ago and had never done it again. The black eye I sported made me the object of speculation in class. That was one of the first times I went to school bruised.

Fixing the cap over her own headwrap, Josephine scrunched her face hideously. I wished she would make that face at me.

Not until the chorus did I realize what the song was—"I Want to Be Bad", the new song by that American girl. I'd heard recordings of it a couple times, but the original singer warbled the notes like a bird. Josephine sang them like a secret, in that husky way of hers.

"*Sleep each morning till after ten...*" This time Henri's voice chimed in, sweet and generous and melodious.

Josephine's attention shifted to me as she finished the line. "*Then the answer is yes, I want to be bad!*"

With a wink, she returned to Henri seated at the piano and drew her long fingers across his shoulders. The notes didn't falter when he turned and gave her a swift kiss. He didn't seem bothered to see Julien's cap on her head. Instead, he chuckled.

When she sidled back over to us, I tried humming the tune and came in on the next *I want to be bad*. That seemed to please her.

She smiled and hauled first Julien, then me, to our feet. Julien looked absurd, shaking his hips as the song instructed, but we'd long since fallen into an in-between space where convention didn't matter. We were safe within a bubble of magic, soon popped, but now soft and glittering.

Josephine's finger trailed down to the top button of my shirt and hooked there, pulling me to her before she let go. I felt light-headed and too warm.

I'd encountered flirtation before, but nothing this overt, especially not from a friend's girl. Would I be attracted to Josephine if Henri weren't already her beau? I dismissed the idea and glanced again at Henri, who seemed to think nothing was amiss. Maybe they'd planned this part too. Now wasn't the time for overthinking.

"*Nobody cares just how blue and how lonesome I am,*" she sang, the song sliding into mock melancholy.

Henri sang the next line lustily, and Josephine gave Julien a peck on the cheek. I laughed. Now that I knew more of the words, I sang along from my lowest note to the top of my range. The song got wilder with all four of us caring less for the tune than for the mad enjoyment of it. Henri played the melody twice.

Afterward, we collapsed. I halfheartedly ate a few more pickles, but the night already turned in on itself, the glittering bubble of enchantment shrinking. My head spun. I felt out of breath for longer than I should have, trying to understand what had happened. My brain only churned out unhelpful repetitions: *That was... something. That was really something!*

When I went to bed that night, I started reading *Aurora Leigh*.

Ophelia, if you could be anything at all—a soldier, a professor, a musician—what would it be?

❧

What an interesting question! No one has asked me that before. I would want to be a botanist. Different plants and flowers have meanings. Did you know that? Some are obvious, like pansies for thoughts or rue for regret, but there are others. I like the meanings, but I like knowing more about how they grow and flourish as well. You know I enjoy growing things, but as a botanist I could understand better how to foster what I have. Perhaps you could find me a book on the subject so I could learn more.

❧

Rainwater slithered down my windowpane and seeped into the rags I'd stuffed into the leaky frame. I sat on my bed hunched over a typewriter, copying from a notebook lying beside me in the streaky light.

After classes, I'd ridden home and only gotten halfway into my pajamas before I hurled myself into this translation (due the next day). Hours had passed since then and I was thinking of pausing for a smoke. The satisfying report of the typewriter keys wasn't sustaining me as it had an hour before. I gripped the blanket draped over my head so it met under my chin, the pose one of determination.

"Laertes!" Julien shouted, entering the room.

I flinched with surprise, then realized he was dripping on the two finished sheets of translation on the floor. "Julien!" I shouted back.

He didn't seem to notice, but advanced on me like a bull at a matador. I let the blanket fall and a cold draft attacked my bare chest.

"Look!" he said, holding something out to me.

My brow furrowed as I took it. "What?"

The damp newspaper wilted in the middle so I had to hold it by the top and bottom edges.

KING HAMLET KILLED! DENMARK IN MOURNING

What can be said in the wake of a tragedy? Certainly the hearts of all Danish people are smarting today from the sudden and unexpected loss of their leader, King Hamlet, who faithfully served as monarch for twenty years.

Palace liaisons informed the press that a poisonous adder attacked the King on the palace grounds on Monday, November 25. By the time physicians arrived, he had already passed.

A royal funeral will be held on Saturday, December 14. King Hamlet of Denmark is survived by his doting wife, Queen Gertrude, and his beloved son, named for his esteemed father...

I blinked rapidly, barely comprehending.

The King dead? But I'd just seen him. He was in good health, and relatively young. From snakebite?

The chill made each particular hair on my body stand up. I set down the paper and wrapped the blanket around my shoulders once more. *Poor Hamlet!* He was so close to both his parents. He couldn't be faring well. Did he have anyone there to comfort him?

I realized Julien was speaking.

"Is everyone else all right?" I asked. "If there are snakes—"

"Laertes, damn it! Are you listening to me?" Julien snatched the paper back.

When I finally looked up at him, his eyes shone wet.

At that moment, the two of us weren't French at all. We were Danish, through and through. I wanted *stegt flæsk* and the bright houses of Copenhagen and cannon fire off the walls of the Kronborg. I wanted to be with Ophelia and Father. Father had worked so closely with the King and for an accident to take him away so suddenly...

The clack of a hammer told me I'd hit a key. I was shaking. I shuffled the typewriter off my lap as Julien continued.

"It can't have been an accident." He cursed, prolonged and creative. "A snakebite?" He grimaced and waved his arms. The paper crumpled in his hand. He seemed to remember himself and smoothed it out. "It can't be. Politicians and pretenders to the throne were always at odds with the King. My father predicted this! If they would just listen to..."

I stayed silent. Although I often agreed with Julien about politics, his family's opinions exceeded the level of mine, straying into radicalism. They guarded their business like feral foxes, and the King usually made decisions favorable to them. Besides, the news still dumbfounded me. I couldn't form my own opinions. We didn't know what had really happened.

Then it struck me.

"I have to go home."

Julien paused his rant. "What?"

"I have to go home. I'm a member of the court." The words felt like they flew at me instead of coming from me. "I have to pledge my allegiance to... the new king."

Pieces slotted into place. The blanket couldn't stave off the cold inside me—grief for the King, whom I'd liked, and distress at what came next. It didn't matter that Julien had ruined my translation. I wouldn't turn it in, nor take the exam in a week, because I'd be in Denmark.

Pledging allegiance to Hamlet.

✤ 5 ✤

DECEMBER: ARRIVAL

It snowed the day of my departure. Just a dusting, but enough to gild everything white in time for the Christmas markets to open. Hand-created trinkets, roasted hazelnuts, and spiced cider in steaming cups filled tented stalls. Garlands graced the arches of the largest. The air felt nipping and eager.

We rode through clouds of our own breath, slowing because of the number of bystanders and shoppers clogging the streets. I viewed the holiday cheer as a poor child might peer through a window at a treat he couldn't have, seeing but not participating.

Henri and Julien agreed to ride as far as the train station with me before they had to go back for classes. Josephine said she felt indisposed and couldn't come. I still brought *Aurora Leigh* for the trip. I was already halfway through, and it had pleasantly surprised me so far.

I remember little about the days leading up to my departure except how surreal they felt. Ophelia, Hamlet, and my father were constantly on my mind. Something about the idea that Hamlet would succeed to the throne after his father's death wouldn't properly penetrate my consciousness. I could answer the question of succession correctly, but then I tried to picture Hamlet as king and couldn't. My heart balked at the thought.

Denmark would love him as their king. He would charm diplomats and ambassadors, and give rousing speeches to applause so riotous it would split the ears of anyone listening. He was an intelligent planner —that would help him too.

I still felt sour because of our row in the summer. Hamlet had many qualities that recommended him as king. Now, though, he would leave Ophelia for sure. And who knew if he would retain my father as advisor?

I gritted my teeth. There was too much, too many things. The Sorbonne (which had to be temporarily abandoned), Denmark in upheaval, my sister brokenhearted, my father's future uncertain, Julien's family dangerously incensed, and time racing furiously on. I would likely not return until January. Already I missed Henri and Julien and Josephine and the past that made more sense than my present. I wasn't ready to pledge my loyalty to Hamlet, unless he made me some kind of assurance of... what? Friendship? Honesty? A show of actual love and marriage to my sister?

Admittedly, I wanted to see what he would do as king. Perhaps the life glowing beneath his skin would burst forth beautifully after all.

The station came into view. The others slowed when I did. None of us spoke. I looked sideways at Henri's profile to see his jaw set in solidarity. In no time at all, our journey together ended.

"Come back as soon as you can, Damon," Henri said.

"Merry Christmas," Julien muttered. "Fuck the bastards. Figure out what happened."

"Say goodbye to Josephine," I replied. "I'll be back when I can and I'll tell you everything."

They left. In minutes, a train flung me toward a country that tasted like dreams.

As we were pulling into Helsingør Port, the captain informed us that there was a disturbance that wouldn't allow us to dock. He didn't elaborate. Perhaps he didn't know the nature of it, but the way his eyes flashed and shifted away suggested it had something to do with the King's recent death. Those in league with Julien's family and their views could temporarily shut down the ports, though I didn't see what goal that would achieve.

The result was more slow, uncertain hours as the steamship changed course and headed instead for Copenhagen.

Standing alone on the deck, I shoved my hands deeper into the pockets of my double-breasted jacket, peering out into nothing but layers of white. Had Reynaldo gotten news of our redirection? Our serving man usually picked me up portside to escort me to the palace.

The mundane question melted away like snow, as though he were part of another life. The world had turned frostily enchanted, a place of fairy lights and sea monsters and memories. Clouds blew past me, riming the exposed skin on my face.

Maybe it was a different world. King Hamlet's death had spun the edges of my reality askew. He was the only king I'd ever known, and now the prince would mount the throne, and who knew what kind of king he would be? How could he lead well when he was rocked by pain? I wished my friends were with me.

The scent of rosemary made my heart thump. I cocked my head as though I could listen for more. Shredded clouds suddenly felt like the tattered dresses of ghosts. I clenched my fists in my pockets and searched for calm. There were no spirits in the mist. She wasn't here. Was she?

I released a breath as something broke through the relentless depth of white, breaking the spell as surely as a magician. The bright colors of seaside buildings read as faded smudges in the fog as we approached the harbor. My chest heaved unevenly as I went back to my tiny cabin to collect my things.

Shortly, we docked and I disembarked with the other passengers.

Smoke tinged with cooking fish laced the air and chased away the earlier apparition of my mother's perfume. Winter fog still blanketed the city, but here it grew wispy enough to see a couple meters ahead. My thoughts returned to Reynaldo. I didn't see him. Others clomped away over the hollow planks with purpose, heading toward waiting cars or relatives. The fingers wrapped around the strap of the bag slung across my body were already growing tight and numb with cold, and still I saw no one I knew.

"Laertes!"

I turned at the familiar voice.

"My boy!" Father exclaimed as he clapped me on the back.

I gave a weak sort of chuckle, disbelieving and relieved to see him all at once. "Father, how are you?" I meant the question. The dimness didn't allow me to see much expression in his face. Had Hamlet retained his services? How was he taking the King's death?

Instead of answering, he herded me off the dock and toward a waiting motorcar. Reynaldo sat in the driver's seat. I got into the back after my father, and our serving man started the engine. Off we drove over the rough streets, heading north.

"You're here," I tried again, twisting to face my father. It was easier to see him now. Drops of moisture sat atop his hair, sliding down in the direction he'd gelled it. "You came to Copenhagen for me." The truth of it was oddly moving.

"Yes, well, my son, my only son," he replied vaguely. "It has been positively electric at the palace, with all that's happened. I wanted to find you for myself."

"Are you... all right?"

"Are *you* all right? You've had quite the journey."

"I am desperate for some coffee."

My father tapped the back of Reynaldo's seat to confirm that he'd heard me. "Then you shall have it! You need a jolt to wake you up before you join the fray. Exciting times. Tragic times."

"Yes," I agreed. I had cried once at The Battlements in mourning, so I could avoid doing so at the funeral. "How is Hamlet?"

"Crushed, and even more so now, I expect. Not to speak disrespectfully, but Lord Hamlet has not recovered from Fortune's buffets. In his place, it would be difficult to maintain composure, being crushed and buffeted as he is."

"It is terrible," I said carefully. I couldn't stray too close to the subject of losing a parent without an icy pall falling between us.

"Don't tell that to the King, when you meet him," my father said.

I knitted my brow. "Why not?"

"'Terrible'? Don't believe rumors. You, of all people, should know to rise above them. Her Majesty the Queen no doubt needed comfort in this trying time—"

"What are you talking about?" Now I was totally confused.

"The quirks of Fortune, the way she's buffeted our poor prince."

"Fewer metaphors, please."

"I'm not using metaphors. I'm saying Lady Chance has dealt a trying hand to Lord Hamlet but hopefully a soothing balm to the Queen."

"Father."

He looked at me then, really looked at me. Lines of surprise and sad tenderness carved into his forehead, as though he just realized something. My breathing shallowed. I wasn't ready for more bad news.

"Oh, my son," he said, "you haven't heard!"

"What?" I clasped my hands together to keep them from shaking. "What?"

"The King's brother Claudius will be crowned Denmark's new king. He married the Queen two days ago."

Time warped around me. The wheels of the car trundled laboriously over the road. Inside the car was a sucking silence. My mind blanked.

"What?" I asked again when I could speak.

"Claudius is our new King. I'm sure he will be quite... values my advice... only so much... seems to love... like his brother." Broken fragments of my father's words got into the part of my brain that could make sense of them.

Hamlet wouldn't be king, at least not for a long time. I would pledge my allegiance to Claudius, instead. Claudius, whom I'd seen casually around the palace my whole life, but no more than once or twice a year. Claudius, who lately was rumored to keep company with the Queen. I doubted he knew my name.

He would be king. Wild suspicions rose unbidden to my thoughts. Did Claudius own a poisonous snake, feed adders through the vents like what happened in that one Sherlock Holmes story? No, no, those accusations were unfounded and ridiculous. Circumstances led me down that path, but my father was probably right. King Hamlet died by accident and the Queen turned to someone she knew. Very quickly. Choosing Claudius above her son and leaving him without a throne.

A couple hours later, the fog gave way to snow. Black lanterns lined the roadway up to Kronborg. Red and white flags fluttered limply at half-mast on the retaining walls, and snow striped the green-domed towers.

We drove inside and Reynaldo stopped the car.

"Clean yourself up," Father said. "I want to introduce you to Lord Claudius before the coronation."

"Isn't the funeral first?" I asked.

"The funeral is tomorrow, and the coronation will be held two days after that."

"May I see Ophelia first?"

Father's face softened. "Brevity is the important thing. I'll report to him that we are here and then send for you when he's able to receive an audience."

I lowered my voice. "Why do I have to meet him at all?" I didn't matter. And I would prefer not to. I wanted a meal and a conversation with Ophelia and sleep.

"I've told him about you," my father replied, "and he's keen to meet such an extraordinary young man."

Extraordinary. I didn't feel extraordinary—I felt like a hodgepodge of everybody I'd ever met, all and nothing at once—but I smiled.

"You are," my father said, as though reading my thoughts.

"Everyone has a moment of youthful indiscretion—so did I at your age —but you are becoming the man I always hoped." He cleared his throat and waved as though swatting a fly. "Perhaps the changes in the palace have made me sentimental. Go! I'll send up that coffee. Make sure to shave before you meet the future king!"

Warmed by my father's compliment, I hurried inside to the suite of rooms the Belleforests occupied. Ophelia wasn't in hers so I went to mine where I shaved off my stubble, combed my hair, and exchanged my overcoat for a dinner jacket. It wasn't so bad wearing a jacket when it was snowing outside. I checked by Ophelia's room again. She hadn't returned.

Reynaldo found me shortly afterwards and gave me an appraising look. His face always bore the expression of someone put out, but who had nothing better to do than go along with our nonsense. The exception was when he saw Ophelia. A little life came into his features as he tried to rearrange them into a pleasant configuration but, having had little practice, the result was unsettling. He bade me follow him to meet Lord Claudius. Together, we headed past festively decorated rooms to a reception area.

Claudius and my father stood talking. Father handled a Christmas ornament hanging amongst some tinsel festooned along the wall. If I knew him, he was creating an object lesson via metaphor. Claudius angled himself away, nodding absently. His brown-gray beard had been immaculately trimmed. He already wore epaulets on his broad shoulders.

"Ah!" Claudius exclaimed, seeing me first. "Here he is." His voice was warm and expansive, a slightly hollower version of his brother's.

"Yes," said my father. "Your Majesty, allow me to introduce my son Laertes."

"The one studying at the Sorbonne in Paris?" Claudius recited these facts as someone else would recite poetry by rote.

"Yes, my lord," I confirmed, wishing Reynaldo had reminded me of the way to correctly address someone in Claudius' position. "Your Majesty" felt premature.

My father addressed him. "He will, of course, ask your permission before he returns, in case you would prefer to retain him as part of the royal household."

My pulse stuttered.

"That's right," Claudius said. "You were raised in the palace, and you must be around Hamlet's age. You grew up with him."

"Yes, my lord," I said, still thinking of the comment my father had made to flatter the new king at my expense.

Claudius continued. "Hamlet's mother is understandably concerned about him. He's all but inconsolable about his father's death. That's all very proper, but all that lives must die eventually, and one day, our own time will come." He made a vaguely religious gesture and glanced upward.

"A wise perspective," put in my father.

Claudius stroked his mustache. "Since you were brought up with Hamlet and are familiar with his habits, I want you to draw him toward pleasures, entertainment, something that will begin to alleviate his melancholy. Denmark has much to mourn but also much to celebrate. Hamlet, as the country's darling, leads by his example."

"I..."

"Laertes is happy to be of service," Father said.

Claudius smiled indulgently. "Very well, then. I believe you'll find Hamlet in his rooms."

"What—now?" I asked.

"Unless that's inconvenient for you."

"No," I said in a daze. "I'll go see him." I didn't know how I was supposed to cheer up Hamlet. It didn't even seem fair that after so little time anyone was trying. In his place, I would have liked someone to cry with me, to tell me that my mother mattered, to sit in silence while we both read, to make me hot chocolate... And none of that would have magically made me happy enough to smile before a nation and tell everyone it was going to be all right. It wouldn't. Not for a while. But hopefully it would be in time.

That reminded me, Father had forgotten to send up the coffee.

Hamlet's door was closed, so I knocked. When no answer came, I tried again, harder this time. The sound helped me ignore my growing fear that Claudius wouldn't allow me back to Paris. I had to go back.

The door ripped open and Hamlet stood there, looking feral. His eyes were red through with veins and his hair looked unwashed. He clearly hadn't shaved in over a week in contrast to my chin still stinging with aftershave. The faint scent of body odor clung to him. A weak yellow stain smudged his crumpled black shirt, unbuttoned to mid-chest. He looked as if he'd been loosed out of hell.

Grief felt so tangible I was afraid.

"Um," I began.

"Playing truant?" he asked bullishly.

"What? No, I came for the funeral."

"Not my mother's wedding?"

I bit my lip uncomfortably. I'd had no time to prepare for any of this. I still barely kept up with the barrage of news myself.

Hamlet sighed and swung away from the door frame. "Come in."

I stepped inside and the smell grew a shade worse. The sheets on his bed were rumpled, books and dishes and clothes in disarray across the floor. I'd never seen the space like this. It reeked of misery. He flung himself into a chair and looked at me expectantly.

"I... I'm so sorry," I said.

He ran two hands through his hair. "Thank you for coming," he said like one exhaled word. "Nobody's come."

"Not even—" I cut myself off before I said Ophelia's name. My eyes landed on a glass with two fingers of water still in it. A half-moon of lipstick smeared the rim. So she had been here to comfort him. I would expect nothing less from her. She'd always been better at compassion than I.

"I'm sorry," I said again. "I admired your father. He was a great man."

Blinking rapidly, Hamlet's expression shadowed from deep grief to scorn to keep the grief at bay. His throat bobbed before he spoke again. "Yes." A thought seemed to cross his mind and his features hardened. "Yes, he was."

"I... um... Would you like to go out this evening? It might be good to get a breath of air."

"Why not?"

"You could... clean up."

A mirthless laugh passed his lips. He ran a hand over his week's growth of beard. "I won't look reputable, regardless."

"I never look reputable," I replied.

His laugh was more genuine then, and my heart eased a little.

With speed that almost made me jump, he twirled up from his chair and began rifling through drawers with manic energy. The task seemed to provide a funnel for his grief, or a momentary reprieve he gripped like a rope over the abyss.

"Seven o' clock?" I asked, edging toward the door.

"Demons couldn't keep me away."

In the interim, I finally got to see Ophelia. She'd been bathing when I arrived, and her hair still shone damp when I knocked at her door. She joyfully emerged to sit in the main room and we drank coffee together, which I finally ordered from Reynaldo. Relief coursed through me to see my sister looking so much like herself. Neither her relationship with Hamlet nor the King's untimely death had changed her beyond recognition. Not that they would. Ophelia was a smart girl, not prone to the dramatics that Hamlet had inherited from his doting mother.

Perhaps it was foolish, but Ophelia was my anchor even more than I was hers, though she protested to the contrary over a delicate sip of espresso. There was much more I wanted to share with her but seven o' clock rushed toward me with speed I wouldn't have considered possible.

When I left, I felt I had said nothing at all and resolved to return soon.

Evening fell quickly—more quickly even than in France, this far north—and the only thing I could think to do with Hamlet was to go to the Christmas Follies, a show I'd attended two of the past three years. It was in Helsingør proper, down a little lane between bright buildings. Hamlet looked like my shadow as he followed me all in black. It was an odd feeling to stand out in any way next to him. I had to admit I liked it.

We talked little as we shuffled through the glaze of snow on the street. Finally, we slipped inside House No. 5, as the establishment was inconspicuously called.

Voices and steam erupted inside, where everything was doused in black-red shadows and yellow lights. Sleek-haired men leaned in to speak to women who mingled among them wearing luxurious coats. The coats were all belted, to be opened during the show. Three large Christmas trees drowned in tinsel graced the stage.

Hamlet and I took a seat at a round table near the back, but the girls still spotted him early. They hovered around us, drawing a finger along Hamlet's jawline and mincing with tiny steps by us, letting one coat sleeve droop to reveal a bare shoulder. Hamlet, usually one to flirt ferociously, acted all but disinterested. Perhaps, I realized with a start, he genuinely liked Ophelia, and if that were the case, it was bad form to bring him here. But I hadn't been thinking coherently.

The show began. Hamlet and I ordered drinks. Even after a couple, which he insisted on paying for, his eyes looked clearer than they had in his room earlier.

Around midnight we stumbled out, murmur-singing our favorite number, arms slung around one another. Then I realized that he'd shifted the words.

"*He is dead and gone, lady,*" he sang. "*He is dead and gone. At his head a grass green turf. At his heels a stone.*"

"You could have rhymed," I joked, sensing the mood turn.

"It does rhyme."

I ran his lyrics back over in my head.

Suddenly, squeezing my shoulder as though he were wounded, he gasped, "Laertes!"

I halted to see if he was hurt.

He looked wildly into my eyes, pupils wide. Bright lipstick marked his cheek. The resulting look would have been comical if he didn't seem so grief-stricken. "I'm *gagged*," he said. "I'm all but gagged. Everything that's happened, and I'm the only one who cares, and I can say nothing."

"You can say what you like," I replied. "You can talk to me." It felt good to be in Hamlet's confidence again, though the circumstances could have been better.

"My father was a great man," he slurred. "Like Caesar, like Hercules." He gestured vaguely toward the sea and I knew he was thinking of the statue there.

"Yes," I said awkwardly.

Hamlet gritted his teeth. "Why did she do this?" He didn't look at me then, but hissed the question. He inhaled anger and then exhaled sadness.

"Everyone needs... some comfort," I said, echoing my father's words.

"She couldn't wait two months," he spat.

I felt we were treading on dangerous ground, so I started walking again.

"She didn't even wait for me to get back."

Something in his voice was so honest that I had to do something. I patted his back. He leaned into me, probably getting lipstick on my jacket. "It's... all right," I said.

"No, it isn't." He straightened. "I know why you're here."

"Hm?"

"They asked you to make me forget." He shook his head. "I can't forget."

I felt an accusation in the statement. "I don't want you to forget. I just wanted you to feel better."

"Noble."

"Really!"

"I meant it."

"Oh."

We lapsed into our own thoughts until we reached the palace.

"No," he exclaimed as we approached the gate that would lead us to the large open courtyard within. "I can't speak my mind in there."

The air was cold and I felt bleary, but I halted. Only a guard or two patrolling the perimeter were in sight.

"I don't know what kind of a king I'd make," he said, lowering his voice. "I can be proud and ambitious. And revengeful."

"Please," I said, hoping he wouldn't take the interruption as insulting, but I was afraid of what he'd say.

He continued anyway. "But I deserve the throne, and she didn't even wait for me. It's like she never loved us." He scrubbed at his face, wiping off the last of the lipstick disdainfully.

My throat constricted. "I'm sure she did." Despite my misgivings, I couldn't say anything against the Queen or Claudius now. If Hamlet was gagged, so was I. The possibility of foul play could never pass my lips.

"She doesn't love anyone," he said, eyes reddening as he looked into mine.

After a moment, we slumped to sit against the palace wall. Snow slowly seeped through my coat and trousers. I blew into my hands, but Hamlet didn't act bothered by the winter cold. It froze me, but this moment felt important.

He hummed a bar of the Follies tune when his voice caught. Heartache twisted his face and he brought his hands up to cover it. His shoulders started shaking.

I sat beside him, stiff with discomfort. Should I say something, ignore him, reach out? Our friendship had been that tentative kind that didn't respond well to emotion. *This damned place.*

Heat prickled at my own eyes too. I knew what it felt like to lose a parent, to feel abandoned, to *feel* like this.

Grief convulsed Hamlet until he was lying in my lap, face still in his hands as he wept.

Totally inappropriate, someone would say. My father, perhaps. Or the whole of Kronborg, which I thought of as its own entity. But there was no one here to tell us that our pain wasn't the right breed.

I laid my hand on Hamlet's shoulder. Warm tears slid down my face as I watched him struggle. Hamlet, the one who rarely struggled, for whom life had been so easy.

We stayed there for what felt like a long time before enclosing ourselves again within the palace. It wasn't until days later that I realized I had forgiven him.

6

DECEMBER: DEPARTURE

The funeral and then (almost immediately afterward) the coronation passed in a blur of fashion and ceremony.

Hamlet still wasn't himself, but my fear for him subsided somewhat. He wore black even to the coronation, and the look on his face was sour, although he kept himself clean and icily polite.

Christmas passed in the margins, quickly, as though we participated in something illegal.

"Here," said Ophelia, handing me a small red box wrapped neatly with string. The two of us sat in her bedroom. We'd been discussing Hamlet's state of mind and I grasped this new topic with eagerness.

"What's this?" I asked, taking the box from her. It felt so light it could have been empty. I shook it near my ear. Only the slightest paper-light shift registered as a sound.

She laughed. "Stop! It's your gift."

"Oh. I have something for you too, but it's in my room." Luckily, I'd remembered to get a small present for her in the mad rush before I'd left France. It wasn't much. My mind had been scattered and my funds depleted after buying the ticket back to Denmark. I had, however, forgotten to wrap it.

"I don't mind," she said, readjusting the shoulder of her dress.

"I'll get it for you later."

She smiled and nodded at the little box. "Open it."

I looked at her warmly and went to work on the knots. Lying in the box, on a bed of tissue paper, were the embroidered capital letters L.B. When I lifted them out, the black letters fit in my palm. Green and gold accents laced the edges. All at once, I realized the handwriting was her own. She'd even sewn a miniature rose of May as the period between the initials.

"Everyone's monogramming things these days," she explained in a rush.

"I love it."

"I wanted to give it to you early so I can attach it to whatever you like. If you have a scarf or a bookbag..."

I gave her a swift hug. "My bookbag. Thank you, Ophelia. I'll get it from my room, with your present."

When I returned, she liked the pearl comb I'd bought her and expertly used it to pin up a lock of long hair by her ear. It was a lovely, old-fashioned style. "How do I look?" She twirled, and her dress rasped gently against the wall beneath her flower boxes.

"Very pretty."

"Father's giving you money, I think," she said.

"That's kind of him." I'd been counting on it, in fact. Julien was the only one of us who made his own money in the summer. Henri and I relied on our relatives, a fact that rankled him more than me. I wasn't sure what that said about me.

Ophelia embroidered my bookbag, I finished *Aurora Leigh,* and on Christmas Day, Father, Ophelia, and I went to chapel. The service was splendid, despite taking place in the cramped confines of the castle near our quarters. Everyone attended. Extra candles lent the space an ethereal glow as we heard about the Savior's birth, which long ago shone light into deep darkness.

Hamlet sat by his mother the Queen but never looked at her. King Claudius sat on her other side. I found myself watching them during part of the service, a peculiar pang in my chest, as though she'd betrayed me too.

A mad thought thrilled through me. Did I have a part in her immediate remarriage? I'd heard that she spent private time with Claudius and said nothing. Should I have? Would that have prevented the worse situation now, with Hamlet close to despair and wild disquiet in the kingdom because of rumors that Claudius and the Queen had something to do with King Hamlet's death? Maybe I could have spoken to Queen Gertrude. She always did look at me kindly...

Warmth brought me back to myself. Seeing my distraction, Ophelia had placed her hand over mine. I blinked and refocused, immensely grateful for her ability to show me compassion at times when I had little for myself.

❧

Every year, a magnificent Christmas tree stood in the main hall of Kronborg Castle, adorned with lights and blown glass ornaments. They kept it up through the new year.

Beside it, Claudius stood, wearing the crown of Denmark. The sight filled me with unease.

Many people, including press, gathered there, making the moderately sized space feel much smaller. A reception, Claudius had called it. Father invited me, so I went. It turned out that I knew few people there, apart from a few court regulars I could barely remember by name. Could the rest of them have declined their invitations in light of Claudius' coronation? If so, that was a bold political move. For a second, I wished I had been so bold myself.

Claudius himself, if he noticed the absences, didn't betray any anger or disappointment. "Thank you for joining us," he boomed, silencing the crowd, who all turned toward him. "The memory of my brother's death is still fresh in all our minds." He gave an incongruous little laugh, thoughtful and private.

I closed my teeth in my mouth.

"Such a strange time. But as much as we grieve, we also rejoice at the blessings we've been given." At this, he looked at the Queen, who beamed up at him from where she'd taken her seat.

Polite clapping filtered through the crowd.

"One eye weeps while the other smiles," he continued. He blinked rapidly, as though clearing away a tear. "I'm glad to be surrounded by wise people like yourselves who freely accepted our union, allowing no shadow to alter your judgment. For all, our thanks!"

In the time it took me to ride from train to steamship to Kronborg, Claudius had married Queen Gertrude. I would not have sanctioned it, if I'd had a say.

The crowd, however, applauded, louder this time.

Claudius raised a jeweled cup. "Let us toast! To the past, may we be grateful for your lessons, and to the future, may we be full of joy!" He drank to the sound of cheers.

I sipped from my glass too, though I didn't feel particularly cavalier. His speech had done nothing to assuage my suspicions. Just that morning, I'd raised doubts about Claudius in my letters to Henri and Julien. Father had found me falconing in the cold, trying to get my mind off things.

"Laertes, your father told me you had a request."

I looked up sharply and found Claudius and much of the little crowd looking at me.

My mind scrambled wildly. What request did I have to ask of the King? I glanced at my father, who stood beside me, but he offered no clue.

"What is it, Laertes?" Claudius prompted. I got the impression he repeated my name so he wouldn't forget it. "You cannot ask anything reasonable and be denied." He smiled indulgently, but faltered when my silence stretched into awkwardness. "Was he mistaken, Laertes, or was there something you wanted?"

It came back to me all at once. "To return to France, Your Majesty. Your leave to return to France."

"Ah!" he cried, obviously relieved. "What does your father say? He's indispensable to me, you know."

I didn't care for the confidential air he was trying to develop with me, but I wouldn't rebuff the notice of a king.

My father puffed out his chest and smiled, light dancing over his gelled hair. "Your Majesty, Laertes has secured my leave to return to France to finish his final year at university. He's destined for great things, but first, he must finish his education!" He delivered the line with too much comedic timing, but I knew him well enough to sense his praise was genuine.

"I have no doubt. He's a remarkable young man," the King agreed. "You have my permission to return, Laertes. And I hope you will decide to return to us and serve the crown in the footsteps of your father!"

My throat felt tight, but I didn't respond. I cared about Denmark, I cared about the crown, and, much more than that, I cared about my family, but I couldn't return here. My great mystical future would have to happen elsewhere.

"And now, my son, Hamlet." The King turned his attention to Hamlet, who leaned insolently against the wall nearest the Queen's chair. He still hadn't shaved.

"Not your son," he said in an undertone. I was close enough to hear but doubted most of the crowd caught it.

The King lowered his voice, so the people around them pretended not to hear, though a marked hush blanketed the room. "How are you still acting so gloomy?" The ostensible tone was caring, but a sharpness lurked underneath.

"When one is in gloom," Hamlet bit out, "it's the only option."

The Queen rose from her seat to join Claudius. From my angle, they hemmed him in as though to keep him from escaping. Members of the press stopped trying to hide their interest and came closer. "You do seem so sad, Hamlet," the Queen said. "It hurts me to see it. At least try to have some fun today."

"*Seem?*" Hamlet's eyes looked nearly black. "I *seem* sad? No. Anyone can put on black clothes and cry and sigh and refuse to eat. Those could *seem*. I'm doing this because I *am* sad. I'm grief-stricken, unlike many others."

Eyes glistening, Queen Gertrude opened her mouth to speak, but Claudius cut her off. "It's sweet that you show so much care for your father, Hamlet, but everyone experiences loss. Your father experienced loss, yet he moved on. To wallow in misery like this shows unmanly grief. Demonstrate some maturity and accept what heaven has willed. Don't continue in this adolescent behavior. You see how it pains your mother!"

I could barely breathe. Stars sparkled across my vision. Images of unseeing eyes and rumpled bedsheets, of pelicans and Ophelia splashing in the surf, colored my mind.

Unmanly grief.

Hamlet looked deadly pale as he glared back at Claudius, rage crackling between them. I felt rooted to the spot, trembling.

How could Claudius say those things unless...

Were Julien's suspicions right? Had Claudius somehow killed King Hamlet for the throne? The hatred in Hamlet's eyes suggested he thought so too.

I loosened my grip on the stem of my glass, afraid of breaking it.

"We love you, Hamlet," the Queen said softly.

I realized I was staring. The King must have seen the crowd's attention too, because he turned around, allowing himself to be heard more clearly.

"We do," he echoed. "I love you as a father. And remember, you are the most immediate to the throne. There is much to celebrate! In fact, I think we would do well to stay together past the holidays. Remain here in Denmark. Let's give ourselves the chance to be a family. Don't go back to Wittenberg."

Cold fear gripped me. Hamlet couldn't go back to university? What if Claudius changed his mind about me too?

Hamlet didn't answer, but his wild, distraught look was back. I wanted to tell him it would be all right, to do something that would soothe his soul, but I had no idea if this would end well.

"Yes," Gertrude said, her body language softening so she and Claudius formed less of a cage around him. "I would like you to stay as well. I need your company here with us." There was grief concealed in her tone that Claudius lacked.

For a long moment, Hamlet and the Queen locked eyes. I knew I should look away, but I couldn't. I lapped up their loving interaction like a thirsty man. Even with their impossible request, I wanted to be Hamlet in that moment.

"I'll stay." Hamlet's voice came out a vulnerable whisper meant only for his mother.

"What a loving reply!" Claudius responded as though Hamlet had acknowledged him instead. He kissed the Queen on the cheek.

When the King and Queen finally moved away from Hamlet, I moved toward him, but I had no words. We leaned against the wall together. My mind flamed. Hamlet suffered. But here, I had to hold my tongue.

Ten minutes must have passed before I breathed, "I'm sorry. I understand some of what you're going through."

"You may have seen the landscape from a distance," he whispered back, "but you haven't gone through it. Denmark lost a great man."

"You lost"—I dropped my voice even lower—"a father. That's what matters most."

The Christmas tree light in our shadowy edge of the room painted him in a sort of fairy chiaroscuro. He dipped his head. "No. You don't understand."

Affronted, I pulled away from the wall. Who was he to say so? After my mother's death hurled me into grief, I'd never fully found my way out again. Sourness rested on the back of my tongue. Was even grief a competition?

"Lord Hamlet. If you please..." A young, blond newspaper man in a tan suit cautiously approached us, pad and pen in hand. He must have seen me speaking to him and assumed the ice of Hamlet's frosty silence cracked enough for others to get in interviews.

I slunk away to join my own father, for whom I felt suddenly grateful.

⚜

This far north, the sun was already setting at two in the afternoon on the day I was meant to leave Denmark.

I found Ophelia in her room, tending the flowers she kept in makeshift greenhouse boxes against the window. She liked variety more than uniformity, if her personal garden said anything. There were herb-paris, rue, violets, fennel, daisies, and rosemary. Ophelia's bedroom smelled a little like Mother when the air shifted.

She'd embroidered a riot of violets on her bedspread.

"I think I'm late already," I began.

"The car can wait," she replied, turning from her flowers with a smile. Uncharacteristic lines spidered from her eyes. She hadn't been sleeping.

I scooped her sideways into a hug. "Try to rest," I whispered. "I know you're worried about him, but he'll be all right."

"I'll take care of him."

"That's not..." But I wasn't sure how to finish. I sighed, memorizing her face. I wouldn't see her for months. "Don't wait so long to write me this time."

"Oh, I won't. You doubt me?"

I leveled a look at her. This bold side of her had previously lain latent but I saw it emerge more and more often. She pursed her lips teasingly in response.

"I'm serious. Please write," I said.

"I will."

"And... Hamlet," I began, with no smooth segue. "Please be careful. I know it's good to have his attention, even... addicting, but I'm afraid with him going through all this tragedy, you're going to want to step in and do anything he'd ask you to do, but, I mean... you can take care of him but don't take this relationship too seriously." I was rambling, and knew it.

She quirked a brow but didn't protest.

Emboldened, I went on. "He couldn't choose you even if he wanted to. He has to think of the nation. His marriage will be an alliance when it happens, and we can't offer him enough. I'm sure he likes you, but don't open your..."—I fumbled—"treasure... to him."

I felt myself go red. I had been about to say *legs* and she knew it, by the round-eyed expression on her face. I shouldn't talk that way in front of ladies, especially my sister. The thought chagrined me. Julien's crassness and my father's condescension couldn't help coming out of my mouth.

Treasure? I tried to compose myself.

"Think of your honor, though, really. Your reputation wouldn't recover if you..."

Now it was Ophelia's turn to level a look at me. Elsa sprang to mind and the pit of my stomach curdled. I wondered how she was. The question formed on my lips, as though women had an endless network among themselves, but I doubted Ophelia knew Elsa personally, so I let the question die.

Ophelia set a hand on my arm. Maybe she sensed my floundering. "I understand what you're saying," she said quietly, "and I'll listen, as long as you heed your own advice."

How much did she know? It wasn't only Elsa, but others with whom I'd dallied, both here and in France.

In the silence that followed, the room seemed to shrink around her as she turned back to tending the flowers. How many options did Ophelia really have?

I hadn't considered it much, but Josephine would be stifled in such a situation, where the only expectations were beauty, obedience, and etiquette. Ophelia's life might as well have been bound in a nutshell, while I had infinite space. I suffocated from too much and she from too little. She *couldn't*. That was her reality.

Perhaps women fell between the mighty opposites of home and nation, crushed without freedom or recognition. It was as though I saw my sister for the first time. She didn't act oppressed. Or was I simply too thick to notice? It wouldn't be the first time I didn't see something right in front of me.

Ophelia couldn't so much as wear trousers without comment. I, on the other hand, had to uphold the family honor, support the women in my life, amount to something that history books would see fit to include. I had to rival Prince Hamlet.

Maybe I'd ask Josephine some questions when I saw her next. I didn't even know what questions, but she seemed to have shaken off the constraints that kept my brilliant sister confined.

Ophelia's nimble fingers pruned the little plants and checked the heating mechanism. She and Hamlet might make a good pair, but he was too volatile and too important. My chest ached for her. Not only was her whirlwind romance ultimately doomed, but she was trapped in Kronborg with a possible murderer. Although there was no reason for Claudius to target her, I couldn't help feeling a stab of panic at the idea of leaving her alone here.

"Ophelia—"

A knock interrupted my thoughts. Without waiting for an answer, my father came in. We'd already said goodbye. Why was he here?

"Laertes, the car is waiting for you," he said, bustling forward.

I gripped the strap of my bag, ready to go. My initials L.B. now graced the upper right-hand corner. "Occasion smiles on a second leave-taking, right?" I quipped.

Father smiled indulgently and held out his hand. It took me a moment to realize there was something in it. Slowly, I took it. A healthy collection of kroner and francs, along with something else. His silver cigarette case.

"There," he said, businesslike. "I doubt the new king will feel slighted if I pass this on, and I think you deserve it, my boy."

"But—"

"Have you ever known me to be wrong?"

I had. "Not really," I answered, closing my fingers around the case. It was a beautiful thing. Its cold, smooth surface brought back the memory of when a company of actors came to Kronborg when I was thirteen to perform *The Pirates of Penzance*. Afterwards, my father, who had acted in university himself, sang "I Am the Very Model of a Modern Major-General" faster and faster, conducting one-handed with the silver case, until we were both breathless with laughter.

"Take it. And with it, be sure to remember these few things. They come with my blessing."

Ophelia watched our exchange covertly. He hadn't yet acknowledged her, though this was her bedroom. My doubts grew deeper, though I couldn't have explained them.

My father's aspect melted into a paternal warmth. "A few precepts, if you will. First, those in Paris are particularly good dressers, so don't forget to present yourself well. Not gaudy, but... rich. Apparel gives a first impression you'll never retrieve."

I knew what he was seeing. Right now, I wore a heavy coat in preparation to leave, but underneath I wore my typical shirtsleeves with suspenders, devoid of waistcoat or jacket.

"Listen more than you speak," he continued. "Avoid vulgarity. I know you have good friends in Paris, and keep them close, but don't waste your money on just any newcomer. And don't start fights."

I wrinkled my forehead. How did he know these things? I felt like a child. Father knew about everything that happened in the palace. I still wasn't sure how he got his information. Reynaldo watched out for him now, but our serving-man stayed in Denmark as far as I knew.

"But"—his eyes twinkled as he leaned in—"if you find yourself in one, make sure you acquit yourself well. End it. Beat the miscreant." He laughed.

I found myself chuckling with him.

He became more serious. "And use this money smartly. Don't throw it around as though the well won't run dry."

I sobered. Normally, I didn't think about money. I just spent where I saw fit. Flashes of absinthe and pastry passed before my mind.

"And most of all," Father said, taking hold of my shoulders, "be true to yourself. If you do that, you cannot go wrong." He looked me squarely in the eyes.

I didn't know what he meant. How could I be true to myself if I was merely an amalgam of ancients and family members and acquaintances? Only my guilt felt like mine, exacerbated by the scent in the room. Any good part of me came from Ophelia or Henri or Julien or Father. Those parts would still exist if I didn't.

"All right," I agreed.

Warmly, Father patted my hand still holding the case and the money. He hadn't used wordplay during our entire exchange, I realized. "May my blessing make you hear these words," he said.

"And, Ophelia," I said, turning back to her, "remember what I've said too."

She made a locking gesture over her heart. "I'll remember."

The corner of my mouth twitched into a smile, despite the turmoil I felt boiling beneath the surface. I hoped they would be safe.

"Go, go!" My father shooed me out.

"Don't forget to write," I cried.

My heart twisted as I finally left Ophelia to her small life.

7

JANUARY

I rang in the new year with the crew of a ship taking me back to
France.

Days later, I found myself back in The Battlements at last. I
touched the skull as I entered, feeling less harried than I had in weeks.
Something niggled in the back of my mind nonetheless. Everyone
gathered that night, cocooned against the cold outside. We'd eaten and
talked of nothing for several hours—my friends seemed to eye me like
some friendly beast they weren't sure how to approach with delicate
subjects—and now we sat in the pleasant, heavy after-haze of late
nights.

"So, you met the satyr?" Julien finally asked, stretching himself out
on the armchair, which barely contained him. His shoulders and jaw
looked tense at the thought of Claudius.

"Yes," I said.

Josephine, cross-legged on the floor before Henri's seat, frowned.
"What's that?"

"King Claudius," Henri clarified.

"Satyr?" Josephine rubbed Henri's calf as she gazed up at him.

I hadn't yet given back her book. I would do it soon. Now, it lay buried under clothes that needed laundering.

"Lecherous goat," Julien offered as an explanation.

Josephine's delicate eyebrows rose. "I thought I'd heard the term somewhere. The curse of reading without the benefit of pronunciation." She looked at me when she said it.

Did she mean I did the same thing? I couldn't think of a word I'd misunderstood like that. I shook my head at her, confused.

"Did he really bed the Queen before the King's death?"

My eyes rounded at her question. "What? I don't think—"

"If he didn't, he wanted to," Julien answered. "The man's a menace. He hasn't been king a month and he's already raised taxes on all businesses. Can you believe that?" He swigged his drink. "Says it's for the military, but I doubt it."

"Are you so sure King Hamlet was a good husband?" Josephine mused.

"Better than Claudius!" Julien replied.

"Well, wives have sense and desire as their husbands do. Maybe she had reason to look for another."

I found myself leaning forward to hear her.

"Men teach us to look elsewhere, more often than not. Their vices give us license. What person, man or woman, doesn't sometimes enjoy... sport?"

At this, she looked at me again, and I felt hot. She caressed Henri's calf, but her gaze didn't leave mine.

I frowned and my seat felt uncomfortable, so I excused myself soon after. It had been a long journey from Denmark.

My dear brother,
You asked that I correspond immediately, so I'm writing this on the evening

of your departure. After you left, Father asked about our conversation. I could do nothing but be honest. At the conclusion, he forbade me from seeing or speaking to Hamlet anymore. He would marry me, I'm sure of it. I sensed a proposal coming any day before this tragedy with the King. Of course, I didn't make so bold with Father, but I'm heartbroken and concerned about the prince, Laertes. You saw how he was. Without a compassionate ear, I fear what he will do. Despite Father's command, I must find some way to convince him to change his mind. He doesn't understand how much we need each other.

I hear that a friend from Wittenberg might be coming to visit Hamlet, and I hope it's true. I hate leaving him alone like this. Perhaps that friend could stand in my place, steadying him in this terrible time. I am forbidden so much as to write him, but he needs a friend, as you were to him at one time.

Pray for us. Life here at the castle feels empty without you.

Ever yours,

Ophelia

❧

Dear Ophelia,

I'm sorry you're distressed. Although I'm fairly certain you'll look back at these events with a certain amount of relief for both your sakes, I know that pain will not be answered so lightly. If I could soothe your aching heart myself, you know I would, regardless of what it cost me.

Let me provide some good news. Henri Garnier commented favorably on your handiwork when I arrived. I wear the letters proudly to class. After some discussion, it appears I may be able to complete my courses on time, despite the recent delay. Classes with Lamord also going well. I had forgotten to tell him I was returning early to Denmark for the holidays, so he was aggravated at first. The additional strenuousness of my lessons has only served to make me a better fencer.

I wish you could be here. The air in Denmark was unfavorably cold when I visited. Be safe and comfortable. Don't go out alone.

All my love,
Laertes
P.S. I think you'd make a tremendous botanist. I wish you could be one. I forgot to say so until now.

৩৫৩

I tied Ophelia's latest letter in a stack with the others and placed it in the drawer below the new bouquet of hothouse roses, white this time. The letter spoke primarily of Hamlet's recent erratic behavior, including how he'd cornered her in our rooms, gripped her wrists, and stared at her with wild eyes before stumbling out. The episode profoundly concerned me, both for Ophelia and Hamlet. Perhaps he'd suffered a real break. He'd certainly seemed on the edge of one when he cried into my lap.

Henri was playing indoor tennis with Josephine, so Julien and I had The Battlements to ourselves. I suspected the couple left so we could vent our frustration alone. Denmark had been the main topic of conversation ever since I returned the week before. Henri and Josephine had contributed, but by now acted lost in in the intricacies of politics, ready to move on to other topics.

"What did your sister say?" Julien asked, coming in from the little kitchen.

"Hamlet's not taking it well. He's... not himself."

"Well, I should think not!" he cried. "I passed a newspaper yesterday that said he was acting strangely. Dressing up and parading around the grounds, spouting nonsense. Not just rumors, then."

I shook my head and swiveled in my chair to face him.

Julien resettled his cap on his head. "Denmark's screwed. My father's furious." He sucked in a breath through his teeth, as though inwardly debating his next words. "He's been talking to people. They're ready to do something about this."

"You shouldn't be saying this to me," I muttered. My connections to the palace were too close. If I had known associates in rebel factions, that could reflect poorly on my own father.

"I swear on my mother Zehra that that bastard killed the King!" Julien cried, smacking the wooden back of my chair. "What do you do with a tyrant?"

"Um..."

"*Flectere si nequeo superos, Acheronta movebo.*"

If I cannot turn Heaven, I shall turn Hell.

Julien's father had deep connections to the working men of Denmark. If they all decided to back a cause, the damage could be catastrophic. I pictured a sea of people, now doing more than causing disturbances at the ports, but lapping up against the walls of Kronborg like tidal waves, crumbling the stone with their power. All royals, I thought, secretly feared the common folk.

"But we don't know absolutely that he did it. The reports said a snake—"

"Fuck that. What a *coincidence* that it only bit the King, and at a time when Claudius was poised to usurp Prince Hamlet and get the throne!" He slumped in a chair by the piano. "It's too bad you're not a detective. You found out nothing from all that time in the palace but what everybody knows already. But don't worry. It's only a matter of time before he slips up, shows his hand." His eyes had gone murderous.

Hamlet was in acute danger if Claudius really did murder his brother for the throne, and he had. My heart couldn't deny it.

My belly twisted. Julien had to be right about Claudius, but was his solution right too? Somehow it didn't feel like it. On the chessboard, I was less than a pawn. What could I do to make things right again?

Dear Lord Hamlet,

I'd start with pleasantries but I know you don't like them. Hopefully it's not too much of an imposition for me to write. I simply wanted to offer you again my condolences and say that I hope you are safe and well in Denmark.

Rumor has it that you have friends staying with you, or a friend, at least. That's good. I wish I could do something more from here to help you in your current situation.

I really don't know what to say. Yesterday, I passed a shop selling risala-mande *and immediately thought of you. Do you remember when we were ten or eleven and you ordered triple the cherry sauce for us all? I still eat it that way. I wonder why the French sell it in January when all Danes know it's a Christmas dish.*

Please be safe. Set your feet in case you need to execute a prise de fer. *The nation needs you whole and sound now more than ever.*

Sincerely,

Laertes Belleforest

***

I woke to the smell of stale sheets and ink. My room lay dark, and I couldn't think what had woken me. Blinking against the gloom, the shape of my bed and the pale moonlight outlining the window came into focus. There had been a sound, or a feeling.

I rolled onto my back. The draft from the window blew my skin cold.

A glint of eyeshine made my heart ricochet against my ribs. I angled up on my elbows, scrabbling for a light. Yes, in the corner, something was looking at me.

A shadow, dark even against the night in my room, stained the corner, then leaked closer, larger. At the top were two eyes, now palely glaring.

I froze as it neared the bed. Blood pulsed in my ears. Layers of darkness fell from it like sheets of gossamer, revealing the figure beneath. I clutched the blankets so hard my fists trembled. I knew what I would see. No, I knew *who* I would see.

The frosty air smelled of rosemary perfume. I wanted to speak, to do something that would change the expression on the phantom's face, which now showed through the ghostly black. She gazed, otherworldly, with accusation and concern. I don't know how she managed to convey both emotions. As before, she wore a nightdress and her hair flowed freely about her shoulders as though she were underwater. Blue tinged her form, and pale light emanated from her.

She didn't speak, but we stared at one another, both unbreathing, for a long time, and I understood. I had to make something right. I couldn't fix Denmark, I couldn't fix Hamlet, but one way or another, I could try to atone for my mother's death.

☙❧

As a child, I imagined hell. It was part piety and part self-indulgence. The idea of it would course along my blood and close up my airways and I just wanted to feel feel feel. Not that I could stop. It was compulsatory. For as long as I could remember, I'd gotten sucked into sensation like a herring in a whirlpool. Morbid fascination took me and wouldn't let me go until I was shaking. With desire, with fear, with joy, with anger—it didn't matter. They took me all the same.

Would I go to heaven? Despite my indiscretions—the women, the gambling, the drinking—the question squatted at the bottom of my consciousness like a troll in a fairy tale, waiting for me to ask for an answer but paralyzed for fear that it would be the wrong one.

In the light of day, my mother's ghost seemed part dream. Was it a dream, a creation of my overheated brain? But then I remembered the other times and I believed again.

That was how I found myself sitting in a pew along the cavernous nave of the Church of Saint-Germain-l'Auxerrois the next morning. Perhaps no book could help me, only prayer. Hadn't Ophelia suggested this?

I folded my hands, every tiny movement echoing like a pebble in a deep cave. Great stone pillars rose up toward stained glass windows, which cast an ethereal purple glow over the golden altar. Perhaps I should have chosen a smaller room—there were several in here, by the looks of it—where my prayers could be more private. The hugeness of the cathedral made me feel loud and small at once, like a child.

Behind me, in the back row, a kerchiefed grandmother sat thumbing her rosary, but other than that I was alone. I sat near the front. Somehow that felt nearer to God.

I bowed my head to begin, but I couldn't find words. "*I'm responsible for my mother's death*"? That couldn't be, and it wasn't perfectly true. "*I'm being haunted by her ghost. The King has been murdered. My sister is heartbroken. Hamlet's going mad. What if I'm going mad too?*"

I sighed deeply, grasping for any thought to ground me and quiet the clamoring voices in my head.

The catechism I learned as a boy intoned solemnly in my mind. I pictured the clergyman who had taught it to me, a skinny, white-bearded man who had seemed so tall. He had a way of flicking from one whisper-thin page to the next that made the paper crinkle so loudly I feared the book would rip.

"And what do you chiefly learn by these commandments?" His voice sounded reedy and rich at the same time.

"I learn two things: my duty toward God and my duty toward my neighbor."

"What is your duty toward your neighbor?"

"My duty toward my neighbor is to love him as myself, and to do to all men as they should do to me."

Something followed about parents, but it had been too long since I'd recited to properly remember it. I twisted my fingers in my lap.

"Our Father, which art in Heaven... I don't know who I am or what to do," I whispered in Danish. My words flew up into the magnificently vaulted ceiling, but my thoughts remained below.

The following silence contained nothing but the tiny click of rosary beads.

"I'm not even Catholic. I'm Lutheran," I continued, looking guiltily around. "But please, Lord, tell me how to help my mother, or to do... something right, not to make a disaster of myself."

It was nearly February. Half the school year was already gone.

When you find loyal friends, hold them close to your soul.

But how could I when The Battlements were a memory? My friendship with Hamlet had basically dissolved over time. Why did I think it impossible that the same wouldn't happen with Julien and Henri?

My eyes stung, the gravity of the past few weeks pressing down on me. In terms of helping the nation, I was inconsequential; in terms of helping myself, I was powerless. I thought of Luc's chemist shop and the chemical burns on his fingers.

"*Are not two sparrows sold for a farthing? and one of them shall not fall on the ground without your Father,*" came the words of Christ to my mind. I was the sparrow, heart beating fast, warm and joyous and directionless, always in danger, engulfed by the wash of sky. "*Fear ye not therefore, ye are of more value than many sparrows.*"

I swallowed thickly. I had no promise of Heaven or of absolution, but the verses I'd memorized as a child came back to warm me like a cup of hot cocoa on a freezing, friendless day.

Perhaps all I needed at this moment was comfort, as a mother might give her boy.

❧ 8 ❧

FEBRUARY

I n the best of years, February was depressing. Tomorrow was Saint Valentine's Day, yet the city lay cold and wet under a metal sky.

More and more magazines gathered crumbs of gossip about Hamlet and his increasingly odd behavior. Ophelia faded from the accounts as swiftly as she had entered them.

Classes went on in murmuring rooms that smelled like pencil lead. My translations had a slightly desperate poeticism about them, as though I could seize the beauty of this time and forge it into something lasting. I took too many liberties with the exact wording, as Julien rightly pointed out. Henri, for all his artistic skill, wrote the most mechanically perfect translations of us all, correct to the letter, but lacking breath.

He and Josephine still spent most of their time together. At The Battlements, the four of us spent more Bacchanalian nights, though I tried to remember my sister's admonition that she would listen to my advice if I'd follow it as well.

The result was fewer gambling halls with trill-voiced girls sitting on my lap when I needed distraction. I was a little better, maybe. But a gulf of conflicting influences commented on my every step. I was young and therefore I should be wild. I was noble and therefore should be a gentleman in all things. I was Danish and therefore should have a strong opinion for or against the current king.

I didn't trust Claudius. His rise had been too sudden. If only for Hamlet's sake, for whom I still felt some loyalty and sympathy at least, I disliked him.

In the middle of that blue month, Lamord announced plans to travel to Demark to show his horses. He would be back in a few weeks. Even my fencing lessons, then, had to go on hold.

The voices rose like sea waters to the back of my throat.

As I biked home, water dripping from the trees into my hair as I rode, a poster caught my eye. It was a stylish illustrated one, meticulously attached to the wall with razor-straight edges. Its cream and brown text read thus.

LES TROYENS BY HECTOR BERLIOZ

FEBRUARY 16—ONE DAY ONLY AT THE PALAIS GARNIER!

And, smaller: COME SEE BLOODY, CARNAL, AND UNNATURAL ACTS AS VIRGIL'S VIVID VISION COMES TO LIFE!

A visibly distressed long-haired woman in a flowing white dress bracketed the words, arms flung across her brow. Presumably Cassandra.

Without conscious thought, I made up my mind. I had enough money left from the gift my father had given me to buy tickets to the opera. The exaggerated emotions and sumptuous sets could be just what I needed to get out of my head, help Julien think of something other than treasonous politics, and finally spend time with Henri and Josephine again.

Entering the Paris Opera was like stepping into a vast palace made of amber. Honey light burned in a hundred candelabras, illuminating the molded walls and grand staircases wide enough for three men to lie across between marble bannisters. The ceiling disappeared in delicate dimness, where the highest of the chandeliers twinkled far above.

Though it was only approaching five in the afternoon, resplendently dressed men and women drifted to and fro, talking quietly. Here, everything echoed.

Henri, Julien, and I made our way up the huge expanse of stairs, past the polished statues of topless women holding out candelabras to light our way, and to our private box. The private balconies stacked one on top of the other like elaborate jewelry tins, lit a sultry red within and sculpted where they faced the main auditorium.

I leaned over the barrier. Heavy red curtains draped across the stage. Anticipation buzzed among the crowd below. *Les Troyens* would begin momentarily.

I wedged my finger between my neck and my collar. The three of us had actually remembered to dress well for this occasion, but I was already feeling hot. As soon as I could, I draped my jacket across one of the plush seats.

"Isn't Josephine joining us?" I asked. "I got her a seat too."

"I don't know," Henri answered, not meeting my gaze. "We argued last night."

Julien bent his tall body over the rail to see how high we were. "Lover's quarrel? She's probably just late."

"Probably," I echoed. That wouldn't be out of character.

Henri merely hummed in response.

In my excitement to get to the opera, I hadn't noticed Henri was more melancholy than usual.

I stepped back and placed my hand on his shoulder. "I'm sure she'll be here."

"The performance *is* six hours long," said Julien.

"*What?*" No wonder it started so early. Hopefully the story caught me up in a whirlwind of passion so strong I forgot where I was. If not,

I'd grow restless. I always felt restless these days, starting one thing and abandoning it halfway through.

Julien laughed at my disbelief.

"Is it actually that long?" Henri asked.

"Very nearly. A lot happens between the Trojan Horse and the founding of Rome."

"I know," I said. "I've translated parts of the *Aeneid* too."

From below came the beautifully discordant tones of the orchestra warming up. We sat. A deep hush palled the auditorium.

Then, with a zip of backstage ropes, the curtains parted. I gasped. The set looked like a miniature Troy, jagged buildings rising up, the layers stacked one on top of the other. The chorus stood on platforms positioned invisibly throughout the city. The highest must have been three stories above the stage.

Beside me, Julien breathed an awestruck curse.

I could easily picture Hector and Andromache, Paris and Helen, Priam and Hecuba, walking those streets. Those were the walls where Astyanax flinched away from Hector's flashing helmet, and where Pyrrhus carved his bloody work. I leaned forward.

The first number began lustily, even gladly, pouring over the audience and filtering up to us. I could just make out the brass section in the pit below. Since I knew how this story ended, there was a bittersweetness to the happy song.

The Trojan Horse, when it rolled into the doomed city, was enormous, twice the size of a man. Sections of it were only wire, so we could just glimpse the Greek soldiers inside.

Act 1 came to a close and Josephine still hadn't arrived. She would love this performance. Perhaps she had a problem with her ticket.

"Excuse me," I said, rising. "Just going to stretch my legs." I took my jacket with me, the slight heft of my father's cigarette case in the breast pocket.

Now there was no one on the stairs and the vast space felt magical or haunted in a way it hadn't before. My polished shoes clicked, reverberating off the stone steps, the luxurious sculptures, the molded ceiling. Muffled through layers of decadence, the opera continued its passionate music.

I slipped out the front door into the dark, the jacket over my arm. Cars and people bustled past in the falling darkness but I couldn't make out Josephine's distinctive form anywhere.

Sighing, I debated smoking a cigarette, but decided against it, turning instead back into the opera house. At the side of the grand lobby, I spied a cloakroom laden with furs. Taking the silver case from my jacket pocket and slipping it into my trousers for safekeeping, I diverted there.

"One jacket, please," I told the attendant, holding it out.

The person startled and whipped around, gazing up through lashes as though ready to run.

"Josephine?"

Her tense stance melted and she exhaled.

Then I noticed the velvet rope attached to stanchions blocking the way. For such a long performance, the cloakroom attendant must have left until one of the intermissions.

"What are you doing here?" I asked, bewildered.

"I'm looking for a coat that's long enough to get me into the opera." She drew her fingers down a lavish mink hanging from a rack.

Understanding dawned. I stepped over the barrier to join her. "They didn't let you in."

She shook her head ruefully. "I forgot to change clothes before I left. As though it should matter!" She modulated her voice to imitate a posh gentleman. "Mademoiselle Roche, I cannot let you in until you change into proper dress."

"I mean, it is the opera." I gestured lamely to my own tie and waistcoat.

She looked at me appraisingly, a wry smile on her dark lips. "Yes, you look very nice." She hooked my elbow and drew me deeper into the cloakroom, through the hanging garments, out of sight of the lobby. "Help me choose one." When I hesitated, she added, "Only to borrow, of course."

I chewed my lip, but finally folded my own jacket on a ledge bearing hats and personal items, and began to help her. "What about this one?" I took a coat of silver silk off its hanger.

"The point is to hide what's underneath." She took it from me and put it on to demonstrate. Her trousers were easy to see, every line of fabric visible. Still, I thought it very becoming. The silver jacket and dark curls at her temples made her look like a movie star.

She handed it back. "No, fur is what I need." A mischievous smile curled her mouth. "You try them on as well. If they can cover you, then they can cover me."

"I don't think—"

"Laertes Belleforest, would you deny a lady?"

The cloakroom already felt muggy, but I could see she wouldn't be contradicted. I humored her, shrugging on a long jacket with columns of soft brown fur.

"So handsome," she proclaimed, touching the top of my unruly hair.

"Will that work, then?" I took it off.

The space among the coats was small, and I suddenly felt how alone we were, how close.

"That might do," she conceded, huskier now.

Something shifted between us. She looked up at me with dark eyes and my skin flushed.

"Well, good then," I said.

She made no move to take the coat.

I should have left. I know that.

"We're not often alone," she said, placing a hand on my chest. The soft pressure set my heart quickening. "And that's too bad. I like you, Laertes."

"I…"

"I've seen the way you look at me, too."

"Uh…"

She slunk closer, tipped up her whiskey and smoke-scented mouth.

I dodged in time, tongue dry as cotton. "Henri. You're with Henri.

I couldn't... I wouldn't do that to him." I held out his name like a talisman against my growing desire.

"Ah," she sighed, leaning back and letting her hand slip off my chest. "He hasn't told you?"

"Told me?" I felt stupid, my mind mostly static.

"We ended things last night."

"Oh. I'm... sorry?"

"Don't be. I found there was someone else I wanted more," she purred. Her eyes grew large and mock-innocent, a net to catch me with.

"But..." Her hands found my sides. My hold on rational thought kept falling from my grasp. "Are you sure? Because, Henri." I'd done impulsive things before, but never at the expense of Henri or Julien.

"He'll be all right. He's strong, and so are you." Her touch found the muscles in my arms.

"I..."

She was pressed against me now, her lips against my ear. She smelled like leather and sweat. "You don't want me?" she whispered, low and raspy.

I did want her. Also, in a way I couldn't parse, I wanted to *be* her.

She guided my hand to her waist, untucking the silk shirt so I could feel her warm skin underneath.

My pulse pounded. "It's over between you two?" I managed.

She nodded languorously into my neck.

My breaths came fast as I felt cautiously upward. When she brought her face close, I sank into her kiss. Her mouth opened under mine, urging me deeper. I responded, growing bolder, tasting her, feeling her. My hand reached her small breast and she gasped, almost a laugh.

She took off my waistcoat and eased the suspenders off my shoulders. It was a signal. I worked furiously at the buttons of her trousers, something intensely erotic in the effort. She was masculine and feminine at once. She didn't amble or lisp like women in the Danish court. She was like a new species.

I eased her onto the ledge and pressed in between her thighs. I was mad, passion's slave. Judging from her encouragement, she liked how intensely I took her.

"Oh," she breathed, her voice low and smoky. "Laertes. Oh, god! Yes!"

In the background, as we finished, the chorus of Troy cried frantically as their city fell.

⚜

I cleaned myself up in the washroom before returning to the upstairs box. I longed passionately for a smoke but I knew I'd already been gone too long. With sobriety came the certainty that I couldn't tell Henri what had happened—not yet. It would look like infidelity, which it wasn't. Josephine flirted with all of us, of course, but we knew there was a line not to cross. Later, we would tell him.

Tell him what? Would our encounter change little about the routine we'd fallen into the past few months? Had it been premature after all?

Though concern tinged the edges of my mind, excitement bloomed there too and relief that I could finally acknowledge my attraction without betraying my friend.

I straightened my waistcoat, checked that my hair was in place, at least according to my standard, and entered. It was like walking into sound. What had been muffled now burst into life. The tenor on stage lamented so loudly that his grief seemed to pierce through my body. It felt good. The set had changed too. Now it was—

"Josephine arrived while you were gone," came Henri's whisper.

I froze. Had she told him?

The seat between my two friends was open for me, and on Henri's other side sat Josephine, swathed in the coat I had modeled for her. She smiled amiably at me.

On the armrest between them, Josephine's and Henri's hands twined together. Cold splashed over me, all blood draining from my face.

"They wouldn't let her in," Julien explained.

"Oh," I managed.

She had lied. And I... I'd...

I barely made it to my seat before slumping down. The tenor's lament washed senselessly over my ears, disconnected from my reality.

I glanced again at their hands, trying to unravel the riddle.

"Where's your jacket?" Julien asked in my ear, a hint of amusement in his voice.

The cloakroom flashed before my mind. The ledge where I'd...

"I don't know," I croaked.

Julien nudged my shoulder. "Are you all right? You look terrible."

"Yes." I riveted my eyes on the performance, but I could still see Henri look over, responding to Julien's concern about me. I burned hot.

I didn't know.

Slowly, rising like a large sleeping animal behind the shame, came anger. How could she betray Henri like that? How could she suggest I do something that would hurt my friend so deeply?

Was I really the rake Hamlet said I was? Why hadn't I listened to Ophelia?

The next few hours were torture. Every time one of our group leaned to speak into another's ear, the intimacy stung. I fought not to flinch. Josephine, two chairs away, looked at me periodically but I didn't look back.

Aeneas and Dido's romantic tryst mocked me. By the end of the performance, I felt shaky and sick with guilt. I couldn't do this. I couldn't do this.

The only solution was for Josephine to break off her relationship with Henri, since it was already rocky.

Right?

But after what she'd done, I couldn't go steady with her. Even my anger felt sad. Betrayal coated me like tar. Her sugared words caught me, but only because I was ready to be caught.

We trundled off into the night after the opera ended. Josephine excused herself with some pretense and I felt the reckless need to call after her. We had to talk. We had to make this right somehow. But she simply gave me an encouraging smile, touched my arm, kissed Henri, and disappeared, leaving me to face the cold horror of my situation alone.

She took the fur coat.

As we rode through the midnight streets, I barely felt the chill, although I'd abandoned my jacket in that damned cloakroom.

They'd never find out. That was how it had to be. And Josephine and I would never be together again. Yes, that would spare Henri and avoid any misunderstanding. I doubted I could face a rift between friends who were my Damon and Pythias.

Paranoia welled up in my bones that the specter would visit me, somehow knowing everything.

I dreamed of it that night in the brief snatches of sleep I found, but saw no ghost. In my thoughts and in my room, I was terribly alone.

❦

A week passed before I talked to Josephine in private. In the interim, I left The Battlements as often as possible, arranging private sparring matches so I could fence. Josephine or one of the others always invited me along, but I couldn't focus, couldn't study, couldn't look Henri in the eye, and by now I know both Henri and Julien suspected that something was wrong. Guilt twisted my bones into a creature I didn't recognize.

"Josephine," I hissed as she touched the door handle, ready to leave as the others had.

She let her fingers slip and turned around. "Finally! Yes?" She stalked forward slowly, like a cat, and I backed up.

"No! Josephine, how could you lie to me? To Henri?" I dropped the last word as though he'd be able to overhear. "How could you?"

"How could *I*?" she repeated, drawing out the word. "Laertes, I like you."

I almost echoed her sentiment but caught myself in time. "But this isn't—"

"If we don't tell them, then we haven't done anything wrong." She shook a cigarette out of its case, far too nonchalant. "We were only having fun."

"Fun? We've wronged Henri."

"I adore Henri."

I shook my head, breathing hard. Anything I used to berate her had to rebound on myself again too. "I can't believe... I would die for either one of them, and now..." Heat prickled at my eyes as the enormity of loss washed over me. "You were starting to be one of us. I even... I even admired you." The confession stung, half-surprising me with its honesty.

Her expression became unreadable, guarded. "They won't find out."

"That's not the point!" I flexed my jaw. "Do you really not care about him at all?"

Her whole attitude had become like someone else, inscrutable and defensive. "I was thinking about breaking things off. He's been smothering me lately." Her tone had a false lightness that felt like armor I couldn't pierce.

I roared with frustration. "But you didn't. You're still with him. And he loves you." I wilted under the weight of my own words. Henri loved quick and fierce, and he'd already endured heartbreak too many times. Weakly, I shook my head again. "We never should have—"

"Please." She lit the cigarette in her fingers and brought it to her lips. "Stop making it sound like I asked you to murder your grandmother." She raised her eyes. "You enjoyed it too."

Now, the memory was so tainted that the ecstasy of the moment had all but been erased. "You can't..."

Puffing out a stream of smoke, she drew herself up, eyes flashing. "I thought it's what you wanted."

"Not like this."

She deflated and gave a weak smile. "See, this is why I like you. You're a good man under there. You care about people. You're more than a pretty face."

Cold misery roiled inside me. She didn't understand. I couldn't live with myself. "I'm not. And you don't like me. Not really."

"I do," she said softly, stepping forward. "I like you very much. My Battlement boys." She raised an elegant hand to my cheek.

I jerked back. "Don't!" Suddenly, I couldn't bear to look at her. If I could have taken leave of myself, I would have done that too. "Get out."

"What are you going to do?"

"I don't know. Just leave, please."

"You're not telling Henri."

"I don't know," I snarled, considering it for the first time. Perhaps it would be better to let him hate me. I certainly hated myself.

Over Josephine's shoulder, the skull leered at me.

"Just go."

After she left, I stood shuddering in the center of the room, fighting back angry tears. Minutes passed before I composed myself enough to go downstairs to visit the chemist.

❧ 9 ❧

MARCH

For two weeks, I carried three things with me at all times: the bookbag embroidered with my initials, my father's engraved cigarette case, and a tiny stoppered bottle.

"I understand there's some danger in using this?" I asked Luc when I bought it.

He raised his scarred eyebrow. "Very much. You'll be careful?"

"Of course. I'm simply conducting an experiment. But I need to know what could happen if I do the wrong thing."

"In the blood, it kills almost instantly, all functions and organs shutting down. Don't get it in your eyes either, like a fool. Against the skin the reaction is milder." He rubbed together two of his deeply stained fingertips. "You probably won't die if you accidentally ingest a drop, but I say *probably*. Call a physician if that happens. And don't mix it with vinegar."

He glared at me with dark eyes. In my heightened state, I thought I saw understanding there, or at least suspicion, but my imagination must have supplied the expression because he didn't come up to The Battlements on the days that followed to check on me.

I don't know how they found out. Perhaps Josephine let something slip.

At the time, I reclined on the roof outside my bedroom, smoking and observing the clear sky. A huge flock of birds with silver wings bent and morphed together like a single entity. I felt as though I were looking up at a school of fish from underwater.

Beside me sat the bookbag filled with my schoolwork, the latest being a comparative analysis of *Faits des Romains* and *De Bellum Civili*. Neither were particularly difficult works. I could cobble something together later.

Those days, distraction reigned in me. The black mood that sometimes took hold, regardless of circumstance, now swathed me permanently in darkness. I couldn't see out. So I sat by myself watching the birds.

A crack sounded as someone banged open a door.

I froze, a startled creature. Instantly, I knew.

Stomping footsteps crossed the floor, getting louder. "Laertes!" Julien shouted.

I snuffed out my cigarette. Peering furtively to the edge of the roof, I decided I had nowhere to run. I had done wrong and had to face the consequences.

"Goddamn it! Where is he?"

A murmured answer that must have come from Henri sent Julien in the right direction.

I forced myself to turn and crawl back through the window. My limbs felt wrong, nerveless and electric at once.

As I dropped to the floor, Julien met my eyes. His large nose purpled with the force of his fury. Behind him stood Henri, pale and drawn.

I needed to say something, but my mouth wouldn't form words. What could I say? "Forgive me"?

Julien threw the cap savagely from his head onto the floor and charged, aiming for my middle. We crashed to the floor.

I defended myself automatically, rolling on top of him to land a blow. Just in time, I pulled myself back from hurting him too badly.

Julien had no such compunction. His large fist crashed into my jaw and sent black-white sparks blooming in my vision.

By the time I had grasped what was happening, his bulk loomed above me, crushing me into the wood floor. I struggled to get free before he punched me again.

"You whoreson little...!" he roared.

"Stop!" I cried, grabbing desperately for his wrists. I didn't catch them, but my effort threw him off balance.

"Stop." The echo made me twist to see the upside-down image of Henri still standing in the doorway, watching us. "Stop, Julien. Don't hurt him."

Julien's hands fisted into the front of my sweater, hauling me halfway off the floor before dismissively dropping me again. Wetness ran across my cheek to my ear. I could barely breathe with him sitting on me.

"Don't hurt him?" Julien repeated, incredulous. He turned his gaze toward me. I'd never seen that look in his eye. It made my breath catch.

"Is it true?" Henri asked me softly.

"Yes." Excuses rose up beside the answer, but I choked them down. I didn't deserve mercy.

My ear exploded in sharp, hot pain.

Julien stood up, glaring.

I hauled myself to sitting, but the room tilted before my eyes like a storm-bound ship, so that was as far as I got. I drew my sleeve over my mouth to wipe off the blood.

"Why?" Henri again.

I pulled my knees to my chest, hesitating. "She told me she'd called things off between you two. I..." My words died in a shaky sigh.

A morbid part of me felt relief at the pain, the truth out at last. But this was an ending I wasn't fully ready to face.

Thick silence fell.

If I'd known a fairy who granted wishes, or even something more dangerous like a witch, I would have wished to undo it all, and if that wasn't possible, I would have asked for forgiveness. Forgiveness was as illusive and impossible as magic. Sparkling and beautiful, it lay across a huge divide that I'd been widening since I was born. I yearned for it, but it would never be. Not for me.

Julien kicked me, sharp enough to hurt but only just. "I hope you're happy," he growled, retrieving his cap from the floor and sweeping from the room.

Henri stayed longer, simply looking.

When I didn't say anything, he left. Discordant notes clanged through the wall soon after.

My dear Ophelia,

I spent the last week looking everywhere for a botany textbook for you, but none of them were in Danish, so I've enclosed ten kroner for the purpose. Please honor my intention and find one for yourself. You can do what Father expects of you <u>and</u> become a botanist as well. I want you to have a full life.

We both, Father and I, want you to be respected and loved. He wants no one to misunderstand what a treasure you are. Lately, I've come to find my views changed from his. Some women have more to add to the world than they're allowed, and I think you are one of those. For the sake of future daughters, do your best to rival everyone in intelligence, compassion, and skill.

But what do I know about being a woman? Nothing, I suppose. It just occurred to me that you haven't had as much encouragement as you deserve. My musings come from love. I love you, my dear sister, more than life.

Tell Father I care for him too, and think of him often. I carry his present with me as a reminder of his love. I confess I struggle to comprehend what he meant when he told me to be true to myself. It seems that my impulses (as you well know) only lead me into trouble. I never meant to be a burden to the family. I hope you both will think kindly of me from time to time.

It's a blessing to have a family like ours. Even those lost to us provide us with memories of a happy home.

Please buy the textbook, kiss our father, and be assured of all my love.

Eternally yours,

Laertes

A few days had passed since Julien and Henri found out about the affair. Neither of them had spoken to me. One night I spent gambling until the sun came up so I wouldn't have to sleep at The Battlements. That day, I crept back when I knew they'd be in class.

Josephine fell out of our lives. Part of me felt relief, but another part grieved. Before the opera, she had injected our lives with the unexpected. She taught me to see what I'd been blind to before.

I stopped going to class. Occasionally, I'd buy little offerings and leave them out for Henri and Julien to find—new sheet music, rare editions of Lucan, pastries. I thought about them constantly, obsessed with the tear in the fabric of our friendship. All I had were dregs. It wasn't enough.

I knew not to go into the living room when Henri played the piano. Intruding on that sacred time would be brutish of me. Inside, I felt hollow, scraped out.

So, I wrote the letter to Ophelia and one to Father as well, which included some similar sentiments. I thought of writing another letter to Hamlet with a plea to make things right in Denmark, but stopped myself. I had nothing new to say. Hopefully, the future of Denmark would be safe for Ophelia.

The stoppered bottle sat on my bedside table. I rolled over on my pillow to look at it. The liquid inside was clear, perhaps twenty milliliters, if that.

Before I could second-guess myself, I unstoppered the bottle and tipped it against my finger twice, leaving two liquid beads. Underneath, the skin slowly bled white, then the spot burned as though I branded it, the pain pitching higher and higher.

My stomach roiled. I exhaled heavily a couple times, as I did before a particularly difficult bout, and sucked the substance off my finger.

My tongue burned immediately, but I lay down, refusing to go out for water or bread to calm it. I thought of Socrates in the Phaedo, taking his hemlock without complaint.

Probably, Luc had said.

Restless with discomfort, I replaced the cork on the bottle. My arms felt heavy and it took two tries before I fitted the cork in the right place. My vision wasn't right.

Breath came too fast now. My mind whirled. *Oh God...* What had I done?

All functions and organs shut down...

At the worst possible moment, there, as I lay on the bed with poison in my mouth, I realized I wanted to live. I wanted to live, even if I had to sleep at the docks and never see my homeland again.

I wanted to live.

My thoughts felt swathed in cotton. Hardly anything got through but the animal urge to fight, to keep going. I felt blindly to the edge of the blankets, where the bed dropped off, and kicked in that direction, forcing my body to the floor. I managed to get to all fours, too weak and disoriented to stand. The door rose far, far away, as though it had moved, the room stretching to spite my efforts. I shuffled waveringly toward it.

I inhaled deeply and yelled, short and sharp, like a bark. The darkness balked at the noise for a moment like water does with oil. If desperation hadn't animated my limbs, I might have laughed. How stupid I must have looked, and how much I deserved what was happening to me, but still, my body jerked frantically against despair.

I heaved upward toward the door handle. Missed and collapsed, shaking. Summoning all my remaining strength, I tried again, with only one arm this time. The door released, but my body was positioned in the way of its opening. It hit my shoulder and fell into dark oblivion, defeated.

⚜

When Hamlet and I were around fifteen, something changed. Maybe that was when I realized our disparity or his unpredictability. Whatever it was, our relationship shifted after that.

Castle staff crowded around a small table in a dimly lit room where Hamlet had laid stacks of kroner, including a few of my own. He rattled dice in his hand, peering around at the onlookers. His carved lips lifted in a smirk as though he were the god of chance before he tossed the two dice on the table. He needed a number higher than nine to win.

The maid closest to him, a woman in her forties from whom I'd never seen such emotion, shook her fists with wide, staring eyes. "Come on!" she cried.

The dots added to three. He lost all the money we'd brought.

Cheers erupted and Hamlet leaned back, tipping his chair dangerously far. He swept up the bills and handed them to the maid, who started counting them and passing them out among the staff.

I caught Hamlet's eye. Had he purposely lost our money?

"More than one way to win," he said, rising and coming over to my side of the table. He wrapped one arm around my shoulders. "There's always more if we need it, right?"

The maids and gardeners and cooks did look jubilant at their victory. My disappointment subsided. Perhaps Hamlet was right.

"Did you know?" I asked.

"That I wouldn't roll nine? No, I haven't added omniscience to my good qualities."

He passed me a cigarette and lit it. Then he thumped the table as though he'd made up his mind and said to those assembled, "All right. Come, come, I am a prince!" Someone clapped, but I didn't think he needed such encouragement. Tapping his foot, he started singing a song of his own design, drivel but catchy. "*Then there's life in it. Come, if you get it, you shall get it by running. Sa, sa, sa, sa!*"

"Too short!" shouted one brave soul I couldn't see in the group.

"Like women's love," cried someone else.

Hamlet laughed, creating five more nonsense verses before he settled down next to me.

A cigarette appeared between his lips. "You don't mind that I gave them your money?" He spoke low.

I shook my head. It was practically forgotten already.

"You know, you're more... *just* than most people I've met," he said.

I attempted to blow a disdainful smoke ring in his face in answer, but I'd never mastered the art. The result was spittier than I intended. "Sorry!" I cried.

He wiped off his face with an unreadable expression. "I wasn't flattering you. Why should the poor be flattered?"

"The poor?" I shot back, unable to stop myself. My warm feelings of a moment before evaporated.

"My original theme was complimentary," he said distinctly. "And I'll return to it. Yes, just."

And then, slowly, he leaned forward and lit his cigarette on mine. The room was dark enough that the glow lit our faces for a moment. In the years after that, we repeated the motion many times; the gesture became second nature, but that first time caught me off guard.

When my father discovered where I'd been, I lied and said Hamlet wasn't there with me. The prince acted thankful that I'd covered for him, but nothing was quite the same after that. We rarely encountered each other at parties. I noticed his mental facilities and vicissitudes more clearly than I had as a child. He'd changed. Hamlet's genius was in words, so he probably could have explained what was happening. I only felt the shift.

❧

I blinked. Cold water clung to my lashes. My clothes dampened my skin, from water or sweat I didn't know. Pain pulsed in my head. What had happened? I groaned.

"He's up. He's up!"

I couldn't see anyone, only, dimly, the ceiling above me.

I want to live.

The memory of poison surged back with such force that I gasped and choked. My tongue felt bumpy and burnt.

An arm eased my aching body upright as I coughed. The mattress buckled lower.

"Laertes! Laertes, look at me."

I squinted but the room blurred out of focus.

"Look at me!"

I tried to obey the voice. Julien's voice. The first, who had realized I was conscious, was Henri.

Julien's big face looked closely into mine. It was his arm holding me up. Sliding my glance away, I found Henri sitting on my other side, wedged up against the wall. Their expressions—as far as I could make out—radiated concern.

I started to cry.

"I'm sorry!" I cried in a voice so hoarse it didn't sound like my own. "I'm sorry!"

Although I could never be forgiven for what I'd done, for what I was, the urge to confess rose up irresistibly.

"I didn't want to worry you. I didn't mean to... didn't mean to ruin everything. It was so selfish of me. I thought she might be lying and I still... I still did it."

The arm beneath me stiffened, but didn't let go.

"It's my fault," I blathered. "I'm a notable coward. Selfish..."

"You were," Julien confirmed.

I didn't quail. "I should have thought of you. I should have had one thought in my damn head. It's more my fault than hers. I... I knew. I must have."

Henri's expression, when I tried to gauge it through my tears, didn't betray his mind.

"Hate me if you want to," I continued. "I understand. I have more vices than you know. More than I even have time to act on." I hiccupped, my whole body shuddering under the force of emotion. "Even as a child... even as a child, I couldn't... I was... I couldn't stop my mother from..."

I'd never talked openly about that, not even to Henri and Julien. They knew bits and pieces, but not the whole story. Apparently, my ugliest, most shameful parts yearned to be known so they came pouring out now. I needed to be hated properly.

"Couldn't stop what?" Henri asked after my explanation petered away.

"She... I see her sometimes. I know it's my fault."

"Your fault?" Julien sounded indignant. "What's your fault?"

"I should have done something. I didn't do anything. I found her and... I couldn't do anything."

Henri laid a hand on my arm. "Didn't your mother die when you were seven?"

I coughed another sob and nodded.

"That's not your fault," he said.

"It is. And why are you being kind to me? I deserve... this." I gestured lamely. The bottle caught my eye. It had rolled onto the floor. The others seemed not to have noticed it.

Julien smacked the back of my pounding head. "You're a fucking idiot, you know that? But you don't deserve this."

"You're our idiot," Henri whispered, as though talking to himself.

"Yes," Julien agreed. "We're angry, and you broke Henri's heart, you bastard, but we'd rather you were alive than dead. Any time." His voice caught. "Any time."

Julien scowled, but his eyes were shining.

"I believe you," said Henri from my other side, "that you thought I wasn't with Josephine when you did what you did." He looked down at his hands.

"Doesn't excuse anything," Julien interjected.

"I know," I said penitently. I was starting to feel hot between the two of them, pressed so close to me. I raked wet hair out of my eyes and shoved my sleeves up to my elbows.

"But I forgive you."

I frowned at Henri when he said the words. He sounded sincere enough, but something like anger caught in my chest in response. "No, you don't."

"I do."

"I don't deserve your sympathy."

"That's not what this is."

"Isn't it?"

Thoughtfully, Henri wiped a finger over half his mustache. Again, I was reminded of a Waterhouse painting. He spoke slowly. "I would rather have imperfect time with an imperfect friend, than some counterfeit of perfection without you."

I sat with the words, trying to take them in.

"He said it," Julien replied. He shook me, but lightly. "If Henri can forgive you, then... Damn it, I have to do it too."

What was happening? I hadn't been falsely self-effacing when I told them not to forgive me. I hadn't forgiven myself, so how could they?

I took my head in my hands, leaning forward so I could support my own weight and Julien could let go. "What about... Josephine?"

Henri didn't answer, which told me what I needed. She wouldn't visit The Battlements again. I'd broken something precious that couldn't be repaired.

"I'm sorry," I said again. The words felt as effective as brass knuckles against a barrage of well-aimed bullets, but they were all I had. "I'm so, so..."

I wept, unable to continue.

Finally, I said, "I think... I think I might be going mad."

"You were always a little mad." Julien's attempt to lighten the mood fell flat.

"I do see her."

"Your mother?" Henri asked.

I scrunched my eyes closed against my palms. "Yes."

"There are more things in heaven and earth than we know about," Henri said soothingly. "It could be anything."

How was *he* comforting *me*?

"It's her," I confirmed. "She looks at me, and..." I didn't know how to go on. Surely, this would be too much for them. I felt split open, like a flayed corpse displaying all the latent disease within. But they deserved to know the truth of me, in all its bizarre shades. "She looks at me, and I know she remembers that day, how I did nothing to help her."

"Nothing to be done," came Julien's brusque response. "Would you have haunted us if you'd succeeded just now?"

"It's different."

"How?"

I pulled my hands from my eyes. "Of course I'd haunt you. I'd pay you back for all those ghost stories."

Julien laughed, surprised.

"And there's nowhere I'd rather be than here." I felt again a lump in my throat. My head still ached sharply enough that my vision blurred, but I could tell I would be all right.

I scooped my friends close, one at each ear, and held them for several long minutes. In the silence, my soul started to patch itself, their strength imped on mine.

For the first time in several months, I slept peacefully.

❧ 10 ❧

APRIL: NEWS

I f I'm honest, I missed Josephine terribly. I turned when I heard
husky voices in class, expecting to see her.

Only one woman attended any of my classes, and she sat well
in the back, never speaking up. I said hello to her once. She shied away
as though I were coming onto her and I felt oddly ashamed for elic-
iting that reaction.

After the news of our affair broke, Josephine did try to talk to me
once. She found me coming out of the Sorbonne one of my first days
back. She feigned nonchalance but the delicate lines around her dark
eyes told the truth of her sadness. I would be devastated too if I lost
the company of Julien and Henri.

A twist of reluctance turned in my stomach. Because I was more
entrenched with them, they forgave me, but only one of us could
survive this betrayal—not both.

"Josephine," I said, failing to keep regret out of my voice as I
reached the green bicycle.

She slipped her hands in her pockets, cutting a silhouette sharp as
an illustration. She wore her mauve silk headdress and a white silk
shirt. "Laertes, you can't hide from me forever."

"I can." I mounted the bicycle.

"Maybe I was beastly," she admitted in an undertone, "but it's because I'm a little in love with all of you. You can understand that, can't you?"

I could to some degree, but I didn't know why she would assume so. Henri wasn't nearby, having gone directly to the Louvre after class. Thinking of him and Julien strengthened my resolve. We couldn't be found talking like this. They would draw the wrong conclusion. I cleared my throat. "This has to be the last time we talk."

She raised her chin, a studied independence clicking into place like an elegant machine. "Well, I won't beg." Her steely eyes locked once more on mine and the column of her throat moved in a swallow.

Josephine might as well have become a ghost in that moment. A past without a future, at least in my life.

I wanted desperately for her to create more freedom, but she'd consumed too much at once, like the serpent eating its own tail.

She touched a curl at her temple with a delicate finger. "I have friends in Nice I've been longing to visit."

"Good." I almost said more. I wanted to say more. Something, perhaps, about timing and how ours felt decades off.

She swept away after that, a nomad ready to find new ground. I didn't watch her go.

For me, routine slipped back into its familiar tracks. Class, fencing, study, Henri and Julien at The Battlements—like breathing in and breathing out. A veneer of melancholy coated me after the incidents of the past few months, but it felt almost warm, like the events of a story that hadn't happened to me.

I looked up from reading *Medea* to find Henri sitting in the armchair across from me, a sketchbook in his hand. He met my eyes immediately, so I knew I was the subject of his drawing.

My focus wouldn't adhere to the pages again after I saw what he was doing. His pencil scratched across the page. I became aware of the odd way I sat in the chair, legs draped across the armrest, book held up to my face. I rolled my neck but didn't move.

Julien, studying nearby, quirked a brow. "Planning revenge?" he asked.

"No," Henri replied absently.

I smiled and tried to return to my work.

❦

I loved Paris in April. Cherry blossoms rushed like pink waves over the city, and the sky matched the coolness of the sea. I took long rides after classes (as long as I didn't have lessons with Lamord) just to breath in the scented air and find roads where cherry branches met overhead like joined hands.

That day, the one that changed everything, was beautiful too.

I had just found—miracle of miracles!—a used botany textbook in Danish and bought it straightaway. Its green fabric cover had faded into beige at the corners and a few pages at the end had fallen out, leaving jagged stubble along the spine. Despite its appearance, the front declared that this book was no more than ten years old. Being very loved often wore out objects more than if they were hated, I mused, starting to form ideas for my next letter to Ophelia. How surprised she would be!

I rode homeward past *bouquinists* with their green-roofed stalls, buoyant with my find. Wind swept like cream around me. The Seine churned past, then beneath, then behind me. I slowed as I turned onto the bustling Rue St. Honoré.

The familiar scent of violet soap mixed with motor oil wafted through the air. I wove past crowds of tourists, feeling friendly and expansive. I begged pardon and finally turned into the alley alongside the chemist's shop, abandoning my bicycle against the wall before heading up. The extra heft of Ophelia's book against my shoulder alleviated weight from my mind. It was good, a bright talisman against the foggy future.

When I opened the door and touched the skull's crown, the atmosphere hit me so hard my muscles tensed. If trombones had started playing an ominous concerto, the effect could hardly have been more intense. Breath squeezed from my lungs as though I were waiting for some horror to jump out. Appalling scenarios sliced through my mind one after the other, relentless. All my latent fears rushed to the foreground.

I inhaled slowly. Nothing was wrong. Everyone was fine. No monster had invaded Paris in the moment it took me to enter the apartment.

Entering more carefully, I slung off my bag, setting it next to a precarious stack of hardcovers leaning against a plush armrest. Flipping open the bag's leather flap, I pulled out the green textbook. It was childish, maybe, but I held it against my chest. It felt hard and reassuring.

My pulse began to slow.

Then, quiet as cats, Julien and Henri emerged from one of the bedrooms. Julien's usually bronzed face looked specter-pale, with brown freckles standing out over his large nose. I'd never seen him that way. Was he angry? Guilty? Sad? The only fact I knew for certain was the depth of emotion. He drowned in it.

Ice washed over my nerves. I could barely hook my pinkies on the cover fast enough to keep the book from falling. My focus shifted to Henri. Intricate lines furrowed his forehead and between his eyebrows.

Julien found his voice first. "Fuck." He scrubbed a hand over his face and resettled his cap. From his pocket, he drew a small square of crumpled newsprint. His eyes glazed as he read, as though he knew the article by heart. "*Denmark's King Claudius requires a new advisor after the mysterious disappearance of his former chancellor, Polonius Belleforest."* A faint flicker as he met my eyes. *"After so much upheaval and tragedy in the Danish court, one wonders how much more the royal family can take."*

"Or has taken," Henri added.

Julien acted as if that were his cue to stop reading. He stuffed the scrap of paper back in his trouser pocket. His jaw flexed dangerously. In seconds, he would explode.

Perhaps I would too. I wasn't breathing.

"I'm sorry," Henri amended. "Would your father have left for some reason?"

"No," I croaked as Julien shouted the same word.

"I told you!" Julien exclaimed. "I can't believe even he... even *he*..." My friend's inability to articulate his thoughts frightened me, sent my mind down glass-shard paths.

Father wouldn't disappear of his own accord. He wouldn't leave a court he loved so much he smothered it...

I didn't move. Color leeched out of the room, leaving a sputtering black and white canvas as though this were all a film. Merely fiction.

"I'm so sorry," Henri repeated.

Father would not disappear. He had to be dead.

Killed.

Killed by whom?

Julien seemed to pick up the detritus of my thoughts, because he said, "My father's contacts said there was a disturbance in the royal suite. A servant had to clean up blood. It was all very quiet. No funeral service."

I tried to swallow, couldn't. Gripped my book tighter. My arms shook convulsively.

"Laertes, that fucking bastard went too far." Now Julien's complexion went dark. It was the look he had before a fight. I'd seen that one. He wasn't looking at me anymore.

The texture of the fabric cover imprinted into my fingers. I felt the boards buckling but couldn't loosen my hold. Words fought for dominance of place.

"I will kill him."

My friends looked at me, one in horror and the other with approval. They could both have pinned me down and I still would have found a way to do it. Claudius the murderer had struck down my father—my foolish, wonderful father, whom I loved, who had high hopes for me to become a better man.

When my mother died, I could do nothing. There was no culprit but the resinous blackness in her soul and my own inactivity. The memory soured.

No tears arose, just a gaping, undisputable hollow and the knowledge that, this time, I would have revenge and make it right.

End it, my father had said. *Beat the miscreant.*

"I'll kill the King," I repeated. Laws and decency be damned. This bloody deed would be answered.

"Then we'll come with you."

Julien's eyes shot wide at Henri's declaration and ferocious excitement covered his face. "Damon and Pythias," he agreed. He gripped my forearm and Henri's in solidarity.

As I looked into their burning faces, my grasp on both the book and my friend's arm tightened into something painful and real and ready.

The three of us left later that day, but the journey to Denmark wasn't quick. My bones ached to move faster, to run, to swim if I had to, but my imaginations were folly. There was nothing to do but wait as the slow steamship carved through the water.

The beautiful and terrible thing about impulsivity was that it left no time for reflection.

I stood once again on the deck looking out. My father's cigarette case dangled from my fingers as I tap-tapped its silver edge against the railing. Today's journey was clear, the cerulean sea churning beneath us to the rhythm of the steam engine. The sound vibrated under my feet. If this planking were to give way, nothing could stop the ocean from swallowing me down into all-consuming darkness.

Tap tap.

I turned my mind elsewhere. Reality was dark enough without these intrusions.

Julien assured me there was no murmur of harm against Ophelia, but the castle harbored a madman. How could I not worry? I had a letter ready in my cabin to send as soon as we docked in Copenhagen. She, no doubt, had sent me a message too, which I'd preempted by leaving so soon. I breathed a prayer for her, half expecting to smell rosemary again as I had in December.

Julien had news of Hamlet too. The prince's mind had been steadily declining since his own father's death, and after this final indignity by King Claudius, his mother sent him to an elite mental facility in England, probably as a protective measure.

Periodicals feasted on news of the prince's ill health. I felt queasy any time I spotted a headline, but Hamlet had made it clear that he didn't want my help. He needed it, though. I thought again of his head in my lap.

Tap tap.

As overwhelming as the waves came thoughts of my father. His life lay in his work, his identity as an infallible advisor. He had helped steer Denmark away from ruin and toward prosperity, and he expected me to be able to muscle nations from their vices too. I couldn't. I didn't have the strength.

At least, I didn't before. Much as I was loath to admit it, Father's death provided an opportunity not afforded me in his life—to do something worthy of the Belleforest name.

To kill a king.

Many thought kings were hedged by divine right, protected by God Himself. This desperate undertaking could damn me eternally.

Deep North Sea water breathed like a sleeping beast. The blood pulsed in my veins.

At the end of some glorious day, to be bold to say I was Polonius' son and *know* he would approve...

I pulled in a sharp breath and released it slowly. The wind from our movement blew my cheeks cold.

It was worth it.

Copenhagen drew closer. There we would rendezvous with Julien's family and use their power to aid me. My only goal was revenge for my father's murder, details of which filtered to us speck by speck, but Julien argued that Claudius' deposition from the throne had to be final as well. The Norgaards needed to be there, he said, to see us through the rocky transition. With Hamlet gone and the King dead, I didn't know who would take the crown, and at that moment that wasn't my primary worry. Others would sort out the rest.

For my part, I had a knife, a foil, and the vial of poison, every weapon I could compass, in my luggage. And I had my friends, both of whom agreed that they would spend another year in Paris to make up for the unfinished semester and lost examinations. Another year at the Sorbonne was the fantastical prize at the end of this mythical quest. We had leapt off a path we understood into the unknown. The present barely seemed to exist in a real sense, let alone the future. I had a purpose, though, and Julien and Henri to help me to it.

Tap tap.

I didn't want to think anymore. I wanted to act. Lines from *Aurora Leigh* sang through my reverie then, sharp as pepper and vinegar.

"I was just thirteen,
Still growing like the plants from unseen roots
In tongue-tied Springs, — and suddenly awoke
To full life and life's needs and agonies,
With an intense, strong, struggling heart, beside
A stone-dead father. Life, struck sharp on death,
Makes awful lightning."

❧ II ❧

APRIL: ARRIVAL

Like Kronborg, the Norgaard residence had white walls and pale wooden floors. Unlike Kronborg, it smelled like garlic flatbread when we arrived and set our luggage in rooms bursting with tasseled pillows. Julien's mother served us supper and mint tea on the terrace.

My memory of that overcharged time is hazy.

At one point, inside, Mr. Norgaard offered us pistols. Julien took his, obviously comfortable with the weapon, but I declined. I felt infinitely more comfortable with a blade, so I chose that instead. With it, I could not only kill but threaten and command.

Henri disappeared during those hours; at least, I know he was there but I can't remember seeing him once after we finished our meal.

There were many, Mr. Norgaard explained, who would follow me in my cause. He would organize the people, and all I had to do was take the revenge I craved.

He fed me with rumors: blood-streaked tapestries, increased surveillance, stores of poison, reason out of tune, dangerous lunacy. I swelled to bursting.

So, when the time came to raid the castle, my thoughts were bloody and will was set.

❧

The cold sun rose behind the Kronborg lighthouse, draping the sky in orange. We hid amongst the buildings across the moat from the castle, facing the Sound. Julien clasped my shoulder. His father stood on his other side, pale face set against the castle with a look of unspeakable wrong, eyes alight. Norgaard sympathizers surrounded us, giving me strength and making me nervous at once. This host of men strained like dogs in the slips in their eagerness.

My shallow breathing didn't deepen at the weight of Julien's hand, but his presence did bring me some solace. He wasn't the behemoth among these men that he was at The Battlements, but he would do everything in his power to make sure I faced Claudius alone to requite him for my father's death.

Henri had stayed behind, ever a man of peace. His presence in Copenhagen felt like an anchor stopping me from flying away or combusting from heightened feeling. A place existed I could return to.

We moved quietly and I felt the silence like delay. It ground against my bones. Scouts in front with experience in the war cleared our path along the berm. We followed it parallel to the moat until the road turned right into the castle courtyard. Our limited cover ran out.

So did we. The courtyard was open. A hundred windows like eyes peered down at us, watching as our boots hit the familiar paving stones. Our raiding party—fifty men or more—now made their intentions known.

A shot cracked the air. Someone cried out but, when I spun, the man didn't look hurt. Another, and I knew that one or more must have found their targets.

I accelerated, forcing myself in front to lead the men to the right entrance. In my peripheral vision, several broke off from the main group, probably to deal with the new armed guards.

"This one!" I cried. Secrecy was over.

The doors quaked under our onslaught. Stories made breaking in sound easier than it was. A strangling mass of bodies ripped and struck at the entrance with horror-inducing power. Someone, somewhere, cried out. Perhaps it was many voices. I expected more gunshots to sound at any moment, but the Norgaards and their confederates had known what they were doing.

A groan sounded across the courtyard and our group doubled their effort.

"Kill the King!" cried a frenzied man beside me. I looked over and couldn't tell if the cry had come from the red-haired man or the man with the pinched expression. Did it matter, when we were all of one mind?

"Down with the King!" came an echoing voice. "Laertes shall be king! Laertes king!"

My skin was aflame. *My name* used to mock Claudius, the King of Denmark. It was inconceivable, a shadow world of impossibility. I was a giant throwing Ossa-Pelion on Mount Olympus to overthrow the gods.

The weight of a dozen men crushed upon me. I clutched the knife, angling it away from the mob. My fingers manipulated the hilt as the bruising heft of bodies pinned me against the cracking door, digging into my back and shoulders. Air gusted from my lungs.

Julien must have noticed my predicament because he caught my eye in the din. He launched forward through the wall of violent flesh toward me just as the doors broke inward with a sound loud as a cannon blast.

I fell inside. Several fell on top of me. I scrambled upright, tossing them off.

"Where's the King?" I demanded of no one in particular. My own knowledge of the palace was greater than the mob's, so my question answered itself as I looked around the whitewashed room. Claudius would likely be next door, where the royal couple received guests and spent much of their time.

A gunshot exploded and I ducked. A man screamed. Not Julien. From behind me, the crowd surged wave-like forward to overtake the two Swiss guards flanking the interior door.

My breath came heavy but I took advantage of the confusion and approached. The unlocked door gave under my hand.

Inside stood the King and Queen. They stared at me, eyes ablaze, wearing all their finery in that clean room as though they hadn't been privy to reasonless murders. As though the King hadn't watched the life leach from my father's eyes.

My terror transformed into hard determination.

"Stay out here!" I demanded, finding Julien again in the melee. "Stay out! Watch the door! Let me do this!"

I whirled and stomped into the room, leaving the booming voice of Julien shouting my instructions behind me.

"Where is my father?" I snarled, stalking forward, brandishing the knife. Maybe the bastard would admit his sins before I killed him.

The door shut, drawing silence and menace into the room that held just the three of us.

"Laertes," the Queen gasped, "calm down." She held her hands out in supplication, but I would not be pacified.

"I won't be calm," I said, pinpricks stinging my eyes as I approached.

Picturing this moment was different than experiencing it. In my imagination, the King quailed under my onslaught as I came on with no hesitation, but now he met me dareful, eye to eye.

In one rapid movement, Queen Gertrude stepped forward, hand still out, and gripped my forearm. Her small hand pinched my skin. The touch brought reality flooding back.

We three stood close now, my blade centimeters from Claudius' chin.

I paused.

Why did I let her stay me? Why did I hesitate?

Am I a coward?

"I am not calm," I repeated, tipping the knife-edge up to tap the King's skin. I was already damned, so I might as well embrace it. "Any drop of blood in me that could be calm shows I am not worthy to be my father's son."

Claudius' chin was set hard. He took a small step out of the range of my knife. I nearly admired his iron nerve.

The Queen's hold on my arm tightened. I could easily have shaken her off, but I stood motionless.

"What's the reason for this?" the King asked quietly, his gaze skimming to where the mob waited just outside.

His question struck me speechless. Was murdering an innocent not reason enough?

"Let him go, Gertrude," he said, a perfect gentleman despite my threat.

Hot blood coursed within me. He couldn't cover the devil with sugar that easily.

"Tell me," he urged, then ordered Gertrude once more to unhand me. She finally, slowly, lowered her hand from my sleeve.

I hated his fatherly, conciliatory tone, as though he knew I wouldn't kill him. I would, be he king or no.

I lowered my voice to a growl. "Where is my father?"

"Dead."

I stepped forward, narrowly missing Claudius' cheek with my knife.

"But not by him!" Gertrude grabbed me again.

My chest heaved with intensity, but I stopped. She had such sadness in her gaze when the words ripped from her that I felt a wrinkle of doubt. My shoulders tensed. I didn't need doubt, but action, revenge.

"Then who?" I demanded. "Don't toy with me. Who killed him? I'll dare damnation to have my revenge. To hell, allegiance!" Though I trembled, my knife did not.

The King widened his arms. How was he so fearless? "Are you so bent on revenge," he said, "that you would harm your father's friends as well as his enemies?"

"Friends," I spat. "To his true friends, I'd give my blood." *Like the pelican*, I remembered.

"Good, good." He actually smiled then. "I'll tell you exactly what happened."

Gertrude looked back at him and the air shifted. Her mouth opened, prepared to protest, and then closed. She knew something, probably the truth.

"Your Majesty," I began, addressing her, "what—"

The door handle from the opposite side of the room rattled.

I sucked in a breath. Guards were coming, and I hadn't killed the King yet.

Gertrude's eyes rounded, and she propelled herself toward the door, to open or shut it, I didn't know. I retook my stance, which had softened in the wake of my infant doubt.

The door opened.

I don't want to tell you what I found there.

The Queen rushed forward, beaded gown rasping against the polished floor, to shepherd out the person limping inside. An un-self-conscious song drifted through the room, accompanied by the smell of earth.

"*He is dead and gone, lady. He is dead and gone. At his head a grass green turf. At his heels a stone.*"

"Ophelia," said the Queen, trying to shield the sight of her from me. "Not—"

"Don't interrupt," came my sister's voice. She wriggled out of the Queen's hold and advanced toward us, still murmuring a melody. In her arms she held her windowsill garden. Dirt spilled out and smeared the front of her white gown. The flowers bobbed as she came on. Her unbound hair looked ratty and her unfocused eyes didn't light on me immediately.

I wavered on my feet, the knife falling from nerveless fingers.

Ophelia. Was it... was this possible?

My feet moved toward her. Eventually her focus found its way to me, but nothing sure.

"Ophelia?" I whispered.

Her singing halted.

My throat ached and eyes burned. I touched her hand wrapped around the flower box. "Rose of May?" The words were barely audible, but she would understand them, if anyone could.

She wasn't jarred out of her state but she seemed to recognize me at last.

With a sloppy crash, she dropped the flowers.

"No!" I tried to catch the window box, but it fell. Soil skidded toward the King and Queen and coated my shoes. *The botany textbook.* It lay in my luggage still at the Norgaards'.

Ophelia looked dully at the mess, unsurprised by its disorder. Movement begged for my attention but I didn't look away. Let the mob enter. Let the King and Queen spring on me for how I'd come in threatening them. Let the world drown around us.

My sister mattered more than any royal, and we were drowning together, mourning the same loss.

I laid my forehead against hers and wrapped my arms around her, caring nothing for the dirt covering her outfit or the mob outside or even the murderer steps away. Her warm, uneven breaths blew against my stubbled chin. For a moment the world stopped and let us grieve together. This was the only funeral we would attend for my father.

"*White his shroud as the mountain snow*," she sang to the same tune as before.

I squeezed my eyes tight.

Her singing faltered. "Sing with me. *A-down, a-down...*"

I knew the words to this new song. Hamlet had invented it as a round. I tried to sing along but didn't get more than a couple notes before my voice broke and I had to clear my throat.

She pulled back, though I still held her loosely in my arms. Dirty blonde hair waved around her face. With a twist, she escaped from my hold and bent down, scuffling in the dirt. Rising again, she handed me an herb with stringy roots still attached. The scent wafted up, striking me as sure as a physical blow.

"Rosemary," she said primly. "That's for remembrance. Always remember. Don't forget."

She plucked another from the muddle on the ground and walked past me. I spun, dazed, to watch her. She approached Claudius and Gertrude, inspected them in her new, absent way, and ripped the plant in half, offering part to each of them.

The Queen took the scrap but the King hesitated.

"Take it," Ophelia ordered, pressing the rue into his hand. Before this, she would never speak like this to anyone but me. Her tone was full and authoritative, long pent up. There was no affectation, but a boldness that bordered on Josephine's.

I moved forward to protect my sister if the King so much as twitched in her direction.

"There's rue for you," she explained. "I would give you a violet too, but they're all gone. My father died and they withered up." She made a fist to demonstrate how the flowers turned suddenly to dust.

Her shoulders shook unexpectedly. I raced to her side. "Ophelia. Ophelia, are you...?" But I had no idea what to say. I ached so profoundly that my soul found new depths to grieve from.

She folded against me, dirty hands against her eyes as she wept into my shoulder. I stroked her hair, working out the knots as Mother used to do when our hair became too unruly. With the other hand, I held the rosemary.

Finally, she exhaled deeply and cupped my face. Soil gritted against my cheeks. An eye-film still separated her from me. "They say he made a good end," she said solemnly, nodding as a child might.

I nodded with her. What else could I do?

From the door where Ophelia had entered came a guard.

My knife no longer lay where I'd dropped it. Had Claudius kicked it away? My mind fuzzed and churned so confusedly that I couldn't remember. As though I'd swum the entire North Sea, my body trembled, exhausted. If the guard took me, I'd figure out what to do later. If he killed me, maybe so much the better.

I stepped away from Ophelia.

"Take her out," ordered the King. "Keep good watch over her this time."

My mouth opened. Claudius wasn't going to order my death? He wanted to put Ophelia in care?

The guard nodded and approached cautiously. I stared at him. Gently, he took Ophelia's arm and ushered her away. She trod carelessly over the fallen flowers as she followed him.

"Where is she going?" I asked in a rush.

"To the wards," the Queen answered softly.

I let out a breath. She would be safe there. This was a break, a psychotic break, not something that would last forever. I would get my Ophelia back. We could be a family again, small and broken, but not destroyed. I had to believe it.

Life seemed to have drained from the Queen. Dark circles deepened in her eye sockets. She looked like a corpse, about to collapse. The King noticed as well and he supported her with an arm. Her fingers dug into Claudius' robes until I could see her knobby knucklebones.

"Go with them, my darling. See that she's safe," the King said to her softly.

She obeyed and followed my sister out with labored steps.

When the door shut behind them, I pressed a hand to my chest and caught a whiff of rosemary. Behind my ribcage, my heart felt overlarge and painful.

"God," I wheezed, "can you see this?" I stared down at my feet, hardly seeing the mess of earth and tumbled flowers there.

"I'm truly sorry," said Claudius, nearer now. He, of all people, was comforting me?

I had thought my desire for revenge was boundless, but it was moderate compared to the all-devouring hunger I felt now. Ophelia couldn't have convinced me toward it more if she'd used all her powers of persuasion. This, her... insanity, motivated me more. I could barely think the word.

But if she'd suspected that the King killed our father, she would have reacted in fear instead of boldness, wouldn't she?

I raised my head, spent.

"Laertes, we grieve with you. Ask anyone here in the palace for the truth. I didn't kill your father. If you find any proof to the contrary, I'll give you my crown."

"Laertes shall be king! Laertes king!"

I clamped my teeth together. His offer couldn't be sincere.

"I know you're a gentleman, your father's son," he continued, "and you wouldn't hurt an innocent man. Find out the truth, and I'll help you however I can to get revenge."

I nodded wearily. The crowd outside would hate me for it, but Claudius was right. I wanted revenge so much I felt penned in by my own skin, but I wanted the ax to fall on the offender, not a bystander.

"Hold to that vow," I said gravely, peering up at him through my hair, mussed and dirt-stained from my moments with Ophelia.

He placed one hand over his heart. He no longer held the rue. "I will."

"Then tell me who it is, so we can kill the bastard."

My anger sparked like electricity between us. I resisted the urge to curl my lip. This was all wrong. Julien and the others counted on me to get revenge. I counted on myself to do it. For once, I had a clear purpose and now I stood temporizing.

Claudius drew in a deep breath, but his eyes glittered with something like excitement. My hackles rose. "Prince Hamlet killed your father," he said.

My ears rang. "No, he didn't," I snarled.

"Look. Ask. Do your own investigation, but do me the courtesy of discovering the truth before you threaten me again." He voice grew deep and regal and dangerous. "In your father's memory, I won't have you imprisoned. He thought you were a good boy and I do too."

It was the Queen's attitude of trust before she left the room that sliced cold ice through my veins. Claudius I distrusted, but the Queen... My throat had constricted so I was unable to respond.

"Prince Hamlet is... unhinged, unsafe," he said, more quietly now. "He hardly resembles the person he once was." After a pause, he added, "Find the truth, and when you're ready, come find me."

❧ 12 ❧

APRIL: PLAN

I requested Henri. Being French and uninvolved in the mob, he was neutral in all this, as neutral a person as I could find, anyway. Really, I just needed a friend like lungs needed oxygen. Together we would investigate Claudius' claim of innocence. Even though Henri had a weak grasp of Danish, I knew it was safer to join our judgments together after looking at the facts. If he came to the same conclusion I did, then we had our man. After the past twenty-four hours, I didn't trust myself at all.

The likelihood that Claudius had killed King Hamlet tainted my opinion of him, but he acted so assured of his innocence in my father's death that I had to discover if he was right.

That was how, two days later, I found myself in the Queen's apartments accompanied by Henri, Queen Gertrude, and four royal guards there for her protection.

I'd never officially entered the Queen's chambers before. The only glimpse I'd ever had growing up in the palace was through closing doors. It lay at the bottom of a spiral staircase of wooden steps leading down from the great hall where portraits hung depicting monarchs of the past (all graced by God).

In the Queen's rooms, a huge fireplace with an ornate mantel dominated one white wall, tapestries hung at intervals, and dark wooden furniture sat heavy in corners. The floral antiseptic smell reminded me powerfully of Luc's chemist shop. A sumptuous four-poster bed with lavish covers looked unslept in. My bed, by contrast, was a twist and knot of sweaty sheets. I hadn't rested in any true sense for a week.

The most surprising feature was the ceiling, which featured bubbles of hand-painted scenes. The half-dressed figures seemed to be gods and goddesses. I recognized Kronos eating his son.

My throat bobbed as I stood over the lightly stained portion of the floor. There were faint brownish stains on the nearby wall as well, as though tea had been spilled over it.

Henri glanced at me before bending down to inspect the bloodstain. He squinted at the floor, then over at a nearby rug. He took the edge between his fingertips and quirked his lips at what he found there. I'm not sure what he was doing, besides playing detective for me.

"Your Majesty," I said, turning to the Queen, whose skin had turned bone-white, "you saw everything?"

"It was an accident," she proclaimed, as she had done several times since we'd entered her rooms. The whites of her eyes shone dull and pink. She pointed to the bed and then to the large tapestry where the worst of the violence had taken place. "I sat there, he stood there, and he wasn't expecting an intruder... He feels terrible for what he's done!"

I didn't let myself be moved. A new coldness invaded me at odd hours. Normally, I was all heat, all *now*, but circumstances dictated that I find where truth was hidden. To talk about my father's murder without crumpling into nothing meant I needed to rid myself of emotion. God evidently helped me with the endeavor.

If Hamlet committed this act, I doubted it was accidental. As Ophelia had described it, Hamlet's madness still left room for his brilliance around the edges. He wouldn't kill an innocent man unless he meant to.

Henri stood, and, as though that had been a cue for the Queen to stand taller herself, she did so, turning her frustrated gaze on me. I tried not to flinch. Queen Gertrude had always looked kindly on me, but now that I had been given leave to investigate her husband and son, motherly warmth—at least in my direction—had evaporated.

The truth was too important to forfeit, though, even for that. Purpose burned through my limbs, tempered by these extra steps I needed to take, but clear nonetheless. I would have my revenge on Father's murderer, who not only stole his life but Ophelia's mind.

I prayed it would be Claudius after all.

The idea that it could have been Hamlet had not pierced my consciousness in any real way. It was a story, the way Antigone or Oedipus were stories. Tragic, but distant. I could shut my eyes, reopen them, and the world would be right again. Not that I had tried. My insides knotted in a tight fist of control. The slightest slip could have me raving like my sister or reaching for the vial still tucked into my bookbag. I couldn't let that happen.

"Where was the King, Your Majesty?" I asked, fiddling with the hem of my gray jacket. I wore the nicest one I had found in my closet. The heat was sweltering, but Father would have liked it.

"Probably his own rooms. We were both returning home from a play, and needed a moment to freshen ourselves." At this, she glared at me accusingly, as though I'd compelled her to disclose something unseemly. I saw Hamlet's bent for drama in her eyes. Obviously, she would have refused to cooperate if not for the King's commandment and her desire to defend Hamlet. "His Majesty came here not long after because he heard a commotion."

"My father." I coughed once and started again. "My father was here to speak with you?"

Her head gave a little uncertain bob. "He was going to serve as a mediator between... me and my son. He had grown"—she searched for a word—"unpredictable."

My gaze dipped to the stain on the floor. The events of that evening came into clearer relief.

Hamlet. Surely not...

I passed her information onto Henri in French. My friend nodded, keeping silent in the Queen's presence.

Swiveling to the guards, I asked, "Were any of you assigned to the King's room that night?"

No one answered me. Heat rose up my neck. I breathed deeply, reaching for calm. I could not break.

"No," one of them finally said.

Henri touched my arm, and we requested leave to be excused to follow the path of questioning elsewhere. Queen Gertrude gladly let us go.

Our inquiries eventually led us to the minister, the one who'd delivered my childhood catechism, who said he'd seen the King in the chapel at the same time the murder took place.

I'd never known the man to lie. In fact, he could hardly get through a story without qualifying his tale for accuracy so many times I felt like rolling my eyes. Did it matter that there were three ships instead of two? Did it matter how the nobleman worded his praise of the sermon?

If the minister said he saw the King in the chapel that night, then that was that.

"What was he doing?" I asked.

"Praying," he replied.

Praying? Of all the... Sweat pooled under my arms in the hot jacket and the neck of my shirt was too tight. I pulled it away from my throat to gulp in air.

The evidence was damning, that Hamlet must be my father's true killer.

Hamlet, my childhood friend.

My thoughts finally built like a cyclone, whirling and whirling and uprooting anything not nailed down. Rage possessed me. I'd tamped down my fury long enough to discover the truth, but the truth ripped at my insides. My arms trembled and I exited swiftly with Henri at my heels. Paris had been his element; Kronborg—fuck everything—was mine.

I had to tell Julien and the Norgaards not to summon another attack on Claudius after their last one failed, leaving two dead. That threat of a new attempt had loomed these two days and I was glad they hadn't done anything stupid after their brief stint in jail, but left me to sort out Claudius alone.

I had to tell the King about my conclusion too. Hamlet had been sent to England, out of my reach. Accident or not, I would take him down, and Claudius was the only one who could bring Hamlet back for his reckoning.

Guards trailed me everywhere I went. Now, in this den of monsters, they felt suffocating. I wanted to scream at them to leave me alone, and to bring in Julien so we three could sit together and curse and drink until we felt better.

"It's him," I told Henri after I'd put a few steps' distance between me and my jailers.

"You're sure?" But he looked certain even as he said it.

I chewed the inside of my cheek and huffed out my nose. I didn't trust myself to respond. I couldn't even look back at him.

"Laertes, I... I'm sorry."

I tossed hair out of my eyes, thought of snow and cigarettes and metal jacks, and hurried on.

***

Dear Julien,

I was relieved to hear that you were allowed to go home after you and your father spent only one night in prison. I should have been there with you. With luck, you've remained nearby. I'm sending this letter to the hotel where we once stayed and I suspect you may be still. I plan to request your presence before the King.

Once you hear the truth of what has transpired here, you'll understand why I couldn't follow your instruction in that instant. I had every intent, and my mission essentially hasn't wavered at all. With Henri's help, however, we discovered that Hamlet used the weapon that killed my father. Stories about his motive conflict, the most prevalent being that when he saw someone in the Queen's room, he assumed it was the King, and struck. That's the story I believe. I have no doubt my father's motives for being there weren't malicious. He always liked taking stock of the castle and those who lived in it.

I hope I'm writing calmly. It's difficult to assess my tone. Remember Horace? Pulvis et umbra sumus.

Ophelia is not well. She has taken our father's death very hard. She is not well at all. I am not well either, and I hope to see you soon at the castle. Your support makes you Damon to my Pythias now more than ever. Henri wishes to see you as well.

Yours,

Laertes Belleforest

P.S. After going through some of my father's things (a ghastly project that I hope not to continue) I have found several suits that look about your size. Let me know if you want them.

I turned over the next three cards in my hand. The Jack of Spades lay on top, just the card I needed.

"Ah, see there?" I exclaimed, glancing at Ophelia sitting across from me. I placed the card atop the pile of other consecutive spades.

She watched my hand as it moved, her expression one I couldn't understand. Did I frighten her? Did she see something I didn't? As if she heard something behind her, Ophelia turned, jerking her head over her shoulder.

I drew in a breath, scenting the air. The only invisible presence I'd sensed lately was Mother. Here in the castle, she might be more apt to appear. But the shades of neither her nor Father had haunted my rooms since I arrived.

I traced Ophelia's eyeline to the rest of the white, sterile sick room, but saw nothing unusual. There was an iron bedframe with a thin mattress and two pillows stacked neatly on top of one another. Beside the bed rose a wide-mouthed lamp glaring invasively down at the covers. A rolling metal tray sat along one wall, rising to hip-height, its only items a cup and a folded square of white sheets. Ophelia blended in, wearing a loose white dress and white gauze around her forearms to prevent her from harming herself further.

At the other end of the room were the small round table and two upholstered chairs where we both sat. Playing cards dotted the table, messier on her end, where she had startled and upset them.

I hated this room. This was all wrong. Didn't someone once say that when sorrows came, they came not as single spies but in battalions?

"So," I said, attempting to swallow the lump in my throat, "don't you worry. I'll make this all right again. We'll be a family however we need to be. You know I love you?"

She couldn't know how much. The sick room hemmed us in like trammeled rabbits, belying the magnitude of my affection. If I could have fed her my blood, as I promised Claudius, I would have done so to make her whole again.

Ophelia didn't look at me but seemed to shrink into herself, listening to something I couldn't hear. The sight made my guts twist.

"Ophelia."

Her slow eyes focused on me. They were drugging her. They must be.

I set down the cards and gently took one of her hands in mine. "You know I love you?"

She regarded me shrewdly, but without the same intelligence I knew. "Listen. Don't interrupt," she said.

I nodded dutifully.

She hummed a few bars, as though trying to find the proper place in the song, but then dropped her head, smiling faintly. Squeezing my hand, she said, "Lord! We know what we are, but not what we may be."

"Mm hm." A memory resurfaced. I reached toward the bookbag at my feet, but she clasped my fingers harder.

"We must be patient," she continued, "but..." Tears glazed her eyes and she shivered. "I can't help but weep to think they put him in the cold ground."

"That's all right. That's all right," I soothed, coming to her side of the little table and wrapping an arm about her trembling shoulders. She wiped her tears wildly, not bothering to hide them. Her cheeks flushed red.

Hamlet couldn't return from England quickly enough. How could he do this to us, especially after the death of his own father? Emotions and voices crowded in, thick and suffocating. The loud *no* and the louder *yes* to revenge. The Norgaards' judgment of my temporary alliance with Claudius. My grief, my all-encompassing grief...

I sniffed hard and released Ophelia, leaning toward my bookbag again. Opening the flap, I drew out the large green volume. Last night, I had carefully pressed the sprig of rosemary between its pages, roots and all.

The textbook felt heavy, but that could have been because I already felt like Hercules holding up the world, muscles straining, defeat inevitable. I'd be crushed.

No. No time for depressive thoughts, although they churned endlessly through my mind. I had to get justice for Father and Ophelia first.

I flexed first one hand, then the other, passing the book from palm to palm trying to work sensation back into them before offering the present to Ophelia. "This is for you. It's a botany textbook."

She stared at the cover. After a few moments, she tapped the design on the front with her middle finger. "Pansies," she said. "That's for thoughts."

"Yes, I remember what you said—"

Behind me, the door eased open. Claudius entered with a nurse following closely behind.

"Laertes," he said, his tone clipped, "I've just received a letter from Hamlet. Join me."

I was on my feet.

The nurse slipped into place beside Ophelia.

"Are the orchids out?" I heard Ophelia ask the nurse as I exited with the King. From the corner of my eye, I saw her clasp the book to her chest.

Yes, let her go outside. Anything to ease the broken parts of her and bring the real Ophelia back. I hadn't realized how desperately I ached to hear her thoughts until the possibility of a real conversation was ripped away.

My guards peeled from the sick room door to trail us. Apparently, they cared less about what I did with Ophelia than with this mercenary king.

I channeled my pain into anger and quickened my pace to walk beside Claudius. His stride was long, even compared to mine.

He led us down several corridors before he apparently found the location he wanted. Together we entered a side room and he thrust a piece of paper into my hands.

"There," he said. "Hamlet's coming back."

My lungs seized. Had the King even had time to recall Hamlet from England?

High and mighty king, read the letter, *expect to see me tomorrow. My voyage to England took a strange and sudden turn. Now I'm returning solus to your kingdom. Hamlet.*

"It's Hamlet's handwriting," I confirmed, looking it over.

"*Solus?*"

"He's coming alone." The word was easy enough to understand that I suspected the King of pandering to my interests.

How did Hamlet get out of the facility? He probably charmed the workers there. "All the better," I said after a pause. "I want to tell him to his face that he did this to me."

The King's lips twitched wryly. "Inexcusable," he agreed.

"Your Majesty," I began carefully, "I heard that Hamlet thought my father was you when he attacked."

"He's a dangerous young man, extremely unstable."

"Then why haven't you taken stronger measures against him already?"

The King sighed. "Two reasons. They might seem weak to you, but they mean the world to me. Judging from your display the other day, I'm sure you know that Hamlet enjoys more popularity than I do. If I were to sentence him to death, or even to prison, popular opinion would erupt. It's already poised on the edge, but I trust that, with time, I can win over even our fiercest detractors. Our response needed to look like care, not retribution. That is the same reason that I didn't take stronger action against your friends as well. I don't need to hand Denmark another reason to hate me or slander my reputation. The second reason I couldn't proceed against him is that Hamlet is the Queen's world and I am a mere satellite." He smiled sadly. "I can't make her unhappy."

I frowned. "Then what do we do?" I didn't care one gram about the King's reputation or even the Queen's heart in view of what I'd lost. I suspected the King earned his reputation fairly, but that was a battle for another time.

"I don't take Hamlet's treason lightly," Claudius said. "Your father was dear to me too, so I have an idea that might satisfy all our needs. Will you let me take the lead?"

The question caught me off guard. He was the King. He didn't need to ask, but extended grace to me when I needed it most.

"As long as you don't try to talk me out of finding justice," I replied carefully, trying not to get drawn in. Claudius was a snake, but he said what I needed to hear nonetheless.

The King beamed indulgently. "Of course not. We'll put all our fears to rest." He indicated a pair of chairs and settled into one. I took the seat opposite.

"A couple months ago," Claudius resumed, "I attended a showcase and there was a French rider there better than any I'd ever seen, as much as I would like to praise the Danes." He gave a dry chuckle. "It looked as if he and his horse had become one entity. He spoke well of you."

"Lamord?" I cried. "Was it Lamord?"

The King snapped in recognition. "The very man! He said he'd hardly met another who could match you in fencing. He's your instructor, yes?"

"Yes," I said eagerly. "He's the best there is." Lamord talked about me? But I missed classes and fought too aggressively. He had said I was improving, though. His compliment warmed my sick heart. The pressure in my head eased fractionally.

"I don't doubt it, after seeing him on a horse. His sense of control is immaculate."

"It is."

"Hamlet heard Lamord talking about you, and of course his instinct was to challenge the man's assertion that you were the best."

That didn't surprise me. To him, everything was a competition he planned to win.

"That is the basis of my idea. Hamlet says he'll return tomorrow. If you follow my plan, your revenge will look like an accident, so Hamlet receives justice and even his mother won't suspect we had any hand in it."

I could guess well enough the first part of his plan, but couldn't see to the end of it. "What do you have in mind, then?" I didn't bother repeating the King's honorific, and Claudius didn't correct me. The sense of power thawed my heart further. I, an advisor's son, spoke to the King like an equal.

Claudius hesitated, and I leaned forward. "Laertes, how much did you honestly love your father?"

My brows lowered. "Why do you ask?" My tone came out angry, defensive.

All the times I'd been dismissive of my father rushed back. He could be a nuisance and often pushed me in ways I didn't want, but I loved him. I still loved him. Did the King know about those times I resented him? But what son didn't sometimes resent his father? Those moments filled me with shame now. Couldn't conflicting feelings coexist?

"I don't mean the question disrespectfully," the King rushed to say. "I wish I had known Polonius better. I just know that sometimes separation causes love to thaw, and if we're going to take action on his behalf, I must know how far you're willing to go."

"As far as it takes. I'm willing to do anything."

"It's all right if your feelings have changed."

"They haven't."

"No need to lie to yourself."

"Listen to me, goddamn it! I love my father. I'll do anything to avenge him. Just tell me what to do!" *I'm willing to kill my friend for it. Is that not enough?* I no longer sat in my seat but stood looming over the King, who looked back at me perfectly at ease. My face felt hot.

Charged energy crackled between us.

Claudius' hands caressed the carved armrests before he indicated the chair again. I lowered myself back into it, still at an inconceivable pitch of intensity.

"I'm glad you'll prove yourself Polonius' son in deeds, more than in words." I couldn't tell if the King was proud of me, or sneaking in a sideways jab at my father. I didn't respond, still spiraling downward from my spike of anger. The King had allowed me more than I ever would have guessed, but I doubted he would brook more disrespect from me.

Claudius leaned forward, conspiratorial, and I matched him, taming my breathing and my trembling hands.

"Hamlet comes home tomorrow," he said. "Here's my drift. We will tell Hamlet that you have come home as well. Everyone in the palace will echo the praises of Lamord and shine your reputation. You know Hamlet well, so you know he will take the bait. We will arrange a fencing match at high stakes. At the match, I'll place an unblunted foil among the rest for you to find and, when you score, you can pay him back for destroying your father."

I chewed the inside of my lip. I could hold my own in fencing against Hamlet, but a stab wound at a match wouldn't look like an accident, nor was the plan foolproof. That couldn't be my only recourse.

"I have poison with me."

Only the slightest flicker crossed the King's face at my pronouncement. I could have imagined the expression.

"In the blood, it's fatal," I explained. "I'll douse my blade with it so I only have to scratch him." Now that my mind had turned in that direction, I thought that would be a more painless death than most. I'd felt its effects myself. Apart from the panic of watching my world slip away, my body had merely closed, slowed, stopped...

I knew what it felt like to die.

The reality of our plan crashed into me like a wave. Talking about revenge was one thing, but taking it—even justified—was something else. Hamlet had been a friend once. Where had those times gone?

I turned my gaze to Claudius, the man he'd attempted to kill when he struck my father. Was I doing the right thing, allying myself to the King? I wanted to see Hamlet suffer for what he'd done, but I was here plotting to take his life. Surely, that wasn't right.

"Yes!" the King exclaimed. "We'll apply it to a drink as well, so if he bests you, our plan can still hold."

If he bests you? I shouldn't have felt so affronted. "He won't."

"It pays to be careful," he replied in a low tone.

I struggled to suck breath into my lungs. My tiny gasps didn't do enough to hide my discomfort.

"If I do this for you," I said, "I need to be able to bring one more friend into the castle."

"If?" Claudius' bright eyes grew dark, dangerous.

I glared back. I was the instrument of my own revenge as well as his. He needed me, not the other way around. Life poured into my bones again at the thought.

"*Because* I'm doing this," I amended. I didn't say that he owed me, but I let the meaning hang like condensation on the air. "Julien Norgaard."

At that, the King's jaw flexed with irritation. "You're trying my patience."

"You can strip him of weapons and keep him under guard, Your Majesty, but I need him."

Claudius' expression reminded me of how he had berated Hamlet at the press event at Christmas. The public wasn't here to salvage my interaction with the King.

I held my ground. There weren't many things I knew for certain, but I knew who was dear to me. My love was fierce but few. For family and my schoolmates, I would undergo the worst kind of torture. *Had*, in various ways.

At last, he reluctantly agreed. We spent a while longer puzzling out the details of our plan. Our confidence grew together, my conscience squashed beneath the mission that gave my life purpose. Killing Hamlet was the only way I could see toward becoming my father's son in truth, and requiting the villain for Ophelia's breakdown. If the system of justice wouldn't do it, then I would.

❧

I need to pause. The next few moments were difficult.

❧

The King hushed me and looked past my shoulder to the door. He had been trying to pry from me the location of the poison. It wouldn't be difficult for a trained guard to find if someone searched my rooms, but I stayed silent on the matter.

I turned to see Queen Gertrude trembling, white as cream. She looked momentarily horrified to see me there. I clenched my belly, bracing. I found I had not far to go to make my muscles rigid.

She laced her fingers together until her skin wrinkled beneath her own touch, red and white.

"Calamity chases you, Laertes," she said finally, shaking her head, weak and disbelieving. Her tone pressed out like hot oil. She raised her blue gaze to mine, and I saw the truth there.

"No," I started to growl, propelled to my feet.

I didn't get further than the first noise before the Queen said, "Your sister's drowned."

"No!" This time the whole word got out, and I made for the Queen. Armed guards materialized as though from nowhere. I gripped the silken collar of her shirt in both hands.

With one eye, I acknowledged that I was surrounded, and dropped the garment. I never meant to hurt her, but she had hurt me, left me wounded and bleeding, infected and alone. This news had to come from the Queen, of all people? Someone who should care? Why did she want to hurt me like this, tell these wicked lies?

"Where?" I spat.

She coughed as though I'd choked her.

My legs held me up somehow, but—true to form—they lost feeling. My body and my mind and my soul needed to be elsewhere, to flash sideways through time to another reality that didn't involve so much tragedy.

No. Not tragedy.

My very being protested. It said *no.*

No no no no no no no no no.

"She was... picking flowers," Gertrude said.

I strangled a sound.

Orchids.

"She was making fairy garlands with them."

I was a child. Ophelia was stringing garlands together, weaving them into crowns and sashes. I refused to wear one in my hair, though the velvet purple petals glowed. She looked like an elf princess, someone from a fairy tale, and I was her prince.

I was...

I was her...

"I watched her clamber up a tree to hang the flowers, but the branch... it broke... over the water."

"Did no one go in?" I shouted.

Tears welled in Gertrude's eyes. The King stood beside us and placed a soothing hand on her upper arm. Everything and everyone disgusted me.

"Why did no one go in after her?" *Ophelia's fine.*

No no no no no no.

"I watched briefly from an upper window," the Queen gasped. "Her clothes were starting to buoy her up." With her hands, she mimicked an air bubble caught in a loose dress. "And she was... she was singing."

This was matter for a play, not for my life. I felt a scream harden in the pit of my stomach, but wouldn't let it out.

"By the time I rushed down to check on her, the dress had gotten heavy and... and had pulled her beneath the water."

I wasn't looking at her anymore. My words came out slowly, one at a time, forced from my lungs by custom. "So, she drowned?"

The Queen nodded, leaning into the King's shoulder.

I, alone, heaved breaths that wouldn't come. I didn't mean to vomit on the Queen, but I barely avoided it.

No no no no no.

Ophelia Ophelia Ophelia. My sister...

No!

"I'm sorry," I choked before making it out of the room, out of sight of the King, to weep.

The poison of deep grief is as potent as anything bottled. But friendship can heal better than absinthe. Which we still ordered, of course, and I drank until I got sick. I longed for a different kind of pain, one that wasn't connected to the loss of my family.

We three sat on the floor of my bedroom together. Henri and Julien read, or pretended to—I saw their gazes flick in my direction more than once—and I absently thumbed the cigarette case open and closed.

Numbness had overtaken my overtaxed soul. My huge emotions seemed to have died in their own excess. Despite feeling that I owed Ophelia and Father my anguish, I couldn't help but welcome the traitorous relief. It certainly wouldn't last long.

As soon as Julien arrived the palace as requested, his surliness had melted. Part of me had been anxious that his hatred of Claudius would overwhelm his friendship with me, but I was not disappointed. Henri, likewise, had stuck by my side, even offering to bet a chunk of his inheritance on the impending duel between me and Hamlet, to make it seem legitimate. Claudius would bet on Hamlet; Henri on me. The Danish bet against the French.

Julien slid a corner of torn paper across the floor to me. I closed the silver case, lifting the scrap to read it. In true Norgaard fashion, it held a dirty, somewhat treasonous poem in Latin. A breath of laughter escaped from my nose.

Julien's expression lightened and he cocked a brow at Henri, whose lips flattened in the suggestion of a smile.

"Well done," I said, handing the poem back.

"Keep it," Julien replied as a generous ruler might do. "Hopefully that does happen to him after all, the bastard. You can gloat when it does. Poetically. And tell him it's from me." He made an obscene gesture, his countenance perfectly serene.

I returned the gesture and pocketed my father's case.

"Really, though," I said, "even if that did happen, even if it *does*"— my eyes strayed to the bookbag, which held the ever-present vial— "do you honestly think I'll survive this?" I waved my hands at imaginary protests. "I mean, I thought I was going mad before, and now..."

I hung my head, drew back a fistful of hair and let it go. "I'll be like her. I know it."

Henri set his book in his lap. "You have every right to feel pain and want revenge. That doesn't mean that you can't find a new way to live, eventually."

I sighed deeply. The stabbing, sickening pain had subsided for now, and I was left with hollowness. Deadness. Not-being. How could I live life anew when my lifeblood was gone, and I could nothing to stop it from seeping away? I couldn't hold my family close enough.

My reality was no longer vast but confined like a stage with few people left on it, pieces moving toward their conclusion. There only remained Hamlet the villain, Claudius the shapeshifter, and I. Perhaps I was the hero. I hoped I was the hero. Henri and Julien took a section of the stage as well, but I suspected they were more a place than players, which I'd soon have to leave before my confrontation.

This was the breath before the climax.

"Ophelia's funeral is tomorrow," I murmured. "It's all arranged." I was going to say that the King arranged it all, but I didn't want to set Julien off. Claudius assured me that he would prepare the service beyond what Ophelia would ordinarily receive, even though there would be only a few in attendance.

"Do you want us to come?" Henri asked.

I glanced at Julien. "No." I didn't want any other potential conflict on my mind besides the one I had to face.

"You sure?" Julien readjusted his cap. "*Amicus alter ipse.*"

Behind us, someone cleared his throat.

I jumped. Every tiny thing seemed prologue to another catastrophe. But what could be worse than what had already happened?

In the doorway stood a shockingly red bag of a hat with a young man under it. Fully half his face made a toothy half-moon grin. The guards must have let him in.

"What is it?" I asked at the same time Julien said, "Who the hell are you?"

The man's smile wavered, then clicked back into place. "His Majesty sent me to meet Laertes. My name is Osric."

He waited for me to recognize the name, but I didn't.

"What, uh, what is this?" Julien asked, waggling his fingers above his head like a rooster crown.

Osric's smile widened impossibly, eyes crinkling. His face was mostly teeth. "Thank you," he said, gingerly touching the edge of the sack he wore as a hat. "I like it too, sir. It's traditional. Are you Laertes?"

I raised my hand. "I am." Some of the tension in my stomach loosened. Osric didn't seem like he was here to relay awful news. "Why did the King send you?"

"Well, sir, I understand you have an upcoming fencing match, and His Majesty wants to ensure you are in tiptop shape. I'm something of a fencing instructor myself, sir." He paused to laugh, although I didn't see the joke. This fellow surely couldn't match Lamord for training, but I could use practice before meeting Hamlet face to face.

"All right," I replied. "What happened to Karl Fisker-Madsen? He's taught me before."

Did he want nothing to do with my plan? Did this Osric even know what I planned to do with our upcoming bout?

"I'm only newly arrived at court, sir, so I am afraid I don't know. Perhaps he caught the revolutionary wildness, sir." For a second, I thought he might cross himself.

I felt Julien stir beside me.

"Shall we start now, then?" I said quickly, rising to cut off any retort Julien might say. "I have... business tomorrow, and Hamlet should be back the day after that, so I can practice today and the day after tomorrow."

"Today! Well!" Osric blinked as though he had something in his eye.

"Is that not good?"

"No, it's perfectly good. I will prepare the space."

"Do you need an hour?"

"No, no, no. Merely ten minutes. Gather your gear and I'll meet you there, sir."

This fop was silly, but I kind of liked him. It was like meeting a friend in childhood, when all you had to do was ask to play. He lived in a different world than the scorching pain of mine.

After he left, I turned to eye my companions, whose expressions were dubious.

"Claudius sends you this popinjay?" Julien said derisively. "Does he want you to win?"

"I'm good enough as it is," I protested. Osric would allow me to practice. I didn't expect him to make me better.

Henri hummed thoughtfully, trundling to his feet beside me. "There are more ways to win than by being the best fencer."

His words echoed what Claudius had said about having a backup plan, and I didn't care for them. "I am the best fencer," I snapped.

I hated this waiting. I couldn't mourn properly without revenge. I couldn't let it permeate my skin and drown me, as I knew it must, until the fire of my rage had burned off. Time cooled my anger, turned it black and bitter and too like sadness. Why couldn't we fight now? And then I could... I could...

Clearing my throat, I went and slung my fencing bag across my chest.

"I didn't mean to bark at you, Henri," I muttered.

"No harm," he said.

I hesitated by the door. Letting the two of them out of my sight constricted my heart. What if death strangled them next? A horrible accident? Or, less urgently, what if I needed them, my fragile heart breaking, and they weren't present to bear me up?

"Look after each other until I get back," I said, allowing a guard to conduct me to the practice room.

✿ 13 ✿

MAY: GRAVEYARD

"Jesus said unto her, I am the resurrection, and the life: he that believeth in me, though he were dead, yet shall he live: And whosoever liveth and believeth in me shall never die."

The minister's words washed over my senseless ears as I watched attendants place the lid on Ophelia's casket, obscuring her face for the last time. Her coffin was wooden, cheap-looking. The movement sounded just like a box closing, wood fibers scraping together before thunking into place.

I couldn't breathe, struggled to keep my entire body from shaking. My eyes had become hot stones in my head.

Some of Ophelia's friends were in attendance, softly crying. The King and Queen were there too. Had they stood beside the makeshift grave of my father, swept away like so much refuse?

Veins pulsed in my forehead and neck. Today was the first of May, so fitting for Ophelia that this funeral felt almost preordained, fated since our births like some Greek tragedy. Even this sylvan area near the castle supported the story-like quality of everything.

The minister's attendants began to lower Ophelia down into the earth. I stood in stuffed silence for a few beats as the straps lengthened in rasping gasps as the coffin dropped.

I realized the minister had stopped talking.

"What else are we doing for her?" I whispered.

His responding look chilled my blood. "The King requested that we do this much," he said, his tone maddeningly pacifying. "Ordinarily, because her death was questionable, she would have been buried in a separate plot."

"Questionable?" I hissed.

"She did not die in peace. All evidence suggests that she took her own life."

"*All evidence suggests* she suffered a mental break and didn't know what she was doing!"

"Regardless—"

"What else are you doing for her?"

Bells sang out from a tower. When he didn't answer, I shook my head, my fingers curled into fists.

Someone touched my shoulder. "Laertes," said the King in warning. I shook him off without a glance.

"Let me tell you," I said, redoubling my focus on the minister, "my sister will be a ministering angel long after you've gone to the other place yourself!"

One of Ophelia's friends inhaled sharply at my words. I'd long since given up speaking in whispers.

Ophelia deserved songs to be written about her, paintings, statues. She deserved tales passed down through generations. Most of all, she deserved to live in all the little ways that made up a life. She deserved to make bread and sew violets, walk along the beach and adjust her son's jacket.

"These are for Ophelia," said a voice.

I turned, chest heaving, face hot, to see the Queen standing reverently above the grave. The attendants had reeled in the straps used to lower the body. The King remained beside me, perhaps to prevent me from breaking the minister's nose.

My conviction about the injustice of Ophelia's death lived in Queen Gertrude's red eyes. She held a bouquet of flowers, some of which I recognized from Ophelia's variegated garden. She tossed them in one at a time.

"Sweets to the sweet. Farewell." She canted her head, composing herself. "I expected to bring flowers to your wedding with Hamlet," she continued in a whisper almost too low to hear, "not to strew them on your grave."

"Don't mention him!" I cried, advancing on her for the second time in a week.

Instantly, two pistols leveled at my chest. I halted.

In the breathless beat of quiet that followed, I heard a tap.

"Did you hear that?"

The Queen's eyes went wide, pupils narrowing. "I didn't hear anything."

My attention turned solely to the grave. The coffin didn't move. No more tapping. But what if...

The undertaker, advancing on it, already held a shovelful of dirt.

"Stop!" I cried. "Stop!"

Stumbling awkwardly, I slid down into the grave. Grit and mud coated my hands and black outfit, got in my shoes, which just fit sideways beside the wooden box. "Let me see her. Let me check," I murmured. I knew I sounded like a madman. I couldn't help it. I didn't care.

I fit my fingernails under the lid of the coffin and pulled.

Dimly, as though through a depth of water, I heard voices impelling me upward.

The lid creaked and split. I shoved the meat of my palm into the space and heaved it off. It clunked into the gap on the other side.

There lay Ophelia. Something about her eyelids struck me most. They looked like white clay. Her hair was the same color as mine, a dirty blonde, but her lashes looked dry and dark. Her arms hadn't moved since the ceremony.

Impulsively, I took her hand, examining her fingernails. Had she called for me, signaled that she still had life in her? They were clean and cold, without splinters underneath. She felt like a rubber figure.

I stood suspended, unable to let go. It was only the two of us here. Someone might pull me out soon, but would that be better? I had let her go outside, after all. My sister, my compassionate sister, wouldn't blame me for this, but someone had to.

My forehead scrunched as I gazed, uncomprehending. What *was* this? Mere days ago, Ophelia could speak loving and witty things. She was supposed to be a botanist. This body whose hand I held was a horrible mockery of the sister I loved.

A rock climbed into my throat, constricting my air. I brought her fingers to my lips, a moment away from commanding the undertaker to begin already, damn him. Bury both of us.

"What is this show?" came a loud voice I knew as well as my own. The mysteries of the universe cracked around me and let the present moment in.

Hamlet was back.

"Why are you treating her funeral like a travesty?"

I hauled myself out of the grave in one leap, in time to see him turn from me to the King, lip snarling. He wore a traveling coat and his normally immaculate hair looked somewhat tussled. He must have come out of the trees nearby. Behind him, another man followed slowly, about our age. He looked Italian and concerned.

"Yes, I'm back," Hamlet announced, marching toward Claudius. "It's Hamlet, the true King of Denmark!"

"You devil!" It's all I could manage. Damn the guns. Damn everything.

I collided with him before he reached the King. We sprawled together on the ground. I was on top of him, squeezing his neck, thumb slipping on his adam's apple. The muscles in his neck felt taut beneath my grip.

A girl screamed.

The ground shifted and I fell heavily sideways. Hamlet had somehow shoved me off him.

"Fuck you!" I roared, lunging for him again. The clay eyelids in the grave sparked like white stars in my vision.

I'd beat his face. I'd kill him for his betrayal.

I reached for him, missed as he hurtled backward out of reach. I had no more words, just animal sounds, just rage.

"Don't do this!" he warned. "I'll hurt you!"

I got one good punch to his ear, he got two to my chest, and then we were pulled apart. The Italian and a guard hauled the prince to his feet.

Two guards stood me up roughly before the King shooed them away, acting as justice incarnate, waving a prison sentence out of existence with one hand. I didn't realize how close we were to the grave until then. Two steps would have landed me in it again.

"Why are you acting like I didn't love Ophelia?" Hamlet cried.

I didn't comprehend him. His eyes were wild and drawn.

"I can keep fighting if you like," he continued, jerking his body out of the guard's grip. The Italian man said something into Hamlet's ear, perhaps to calm him, but he wouldn't be calmed. "I'll fight until we can't stand anymore just to prove how much I loved her. You couldn't have loved her more than I did."

I flung myself forward but was yanked back again.

"He's mad, Laertes," the Queen said privately. I thought of the stain on her bedroom floor. Then, louder, to the amazed group, "In a moment, he'll be fine."

Stunned to silence, I couldn't respond.

"What would you do to prove your love?" Hamlet ranted on. His gaze shifted down to the grave, then back up at me. "I'd do anything, and yet you attack as soon as you see me. I'd weep, I'd hurt myself, I'd eat a crocodile if I had to. Let's all be buried, then, shall we?"

I'd never seen him in this mood. Even unarmed, he seemed a weapon. My body responded as though he were one, apt to fire at any second.

He approached, untethered. Had his companion goaded him on?

Still restrained, I took a step back, then cursed myself for doing it.

We were one step from the grave now. I didn't want Ophelia to see us fighting like this. (The thought crossed my mind before I realized how nonsensical it was.)

Some of the violence left Hamlet's stance. He met my eyes, brow furrowed. "Why are you acting like this?" he asked.

Because I'm losing my mind. I almost said it, but held back. The better answer was that he was my father's murderer, but, looking at him now, the Hamlet I had conjured in my imagination seemed like a different person. I'd drunk with this Hamlet, comforted him, lied for him. His betrayal was as confusing as death.

"I always loved you," he said next.

I frowned at the remark and the casual way he threw it into the air like gunpowder. He'd use the same cadence to speak to a servant or a horse. I opened my mouth to speak.

"But it doesn't matter," he said, shutting his eyes. "I'm headed back to Kronborg." With a wave of his arm, he swept from the gravesite, shoulders hunched. The Italian accompanied him. Then I remembered one of Ophelia's letters describing Hamlet's friend from school. That must be Horatio, still glued to Hamlet's side despite his violent unpredictability.

What just happened?

The King drew me a few steps away to speak privately. "Be patient," he said. His breath felt hot against my bruised cheek. When had Hamlet hit me there? "Remember our conversation. We'll push our plan into motion today." He nodded back over his shoulder. "I'll also direct a larger monument to be built on this grave. Your sister's final memory should not be tainted with such senseless violence."

I pressed my lips together tightly as though they were the doorway to my sorrow.

"An hour of quiet," he concluded, "and then we proceed as planned."

Dear Laertes,

I wouldn't have bothered to write, except that I don't know if my Battlement Boys are speaking to each other. I hope so.

The news coming out of Denmark is startling, far too riddled with the name Belleforest. Maybe that's a common name there, but I suspect that it isn't and that your family is in trouble. I'm too far out from Paris to get the really good papers now, but even the bits I manage to scrounge don't tell a happy story. I'm sending this letter to Denmark assuming that you've returned there. I hope this reaches you.

Perhaps you'd prefer never to hear from me again. If that's so, I'm sorry (not very, but a little.) My point is that I hope you're all right. Know that you have a friend in France if nowhere else.

George Sand says, "Whoever has loved knows all that life contains of sorrow and joy." Grief, which I know you must be experiencing, alone or together with Henri and Julien, proves your love. Let no one shame you for it. Your heart was always my favorite part of you. But the last thing you need is for me to speak of the past. I'm sure you've figured out by now that I'm a bundle of disasters.

So, that's everything I'll say. I'm sorry you've fallen on more difficult times. I've included my return address in case you need me, but I won't expect a response.

Sincerely yours,

Josephine Roche

I tucked the letter away in my bookbag, between copies of Voltaire and Livy. A stripe of morning light stained their spines gold-white. I wouldn't open those books until next autumn, if I opened them at all. Neither would Julien and Henri. Besides the cost of another year of university, my family's tragedy had set back their futures as well as my own. Another thing to feel guilty about, though they protested that we would live and die together.

For the sake of honesty, I had showed Josephine's letter to Henri, who read it stoically. It was good to hear from her in such an innocent way, but I knew her note should have bothered or encouraged me more than it did. Instead, I kept thinking about Ophelia's cold hands and Hamlet's cold eyes.

As I replaced the leather flap, I ran my thumb over the initials Ophelia had embroidered me for Christmas. Laertes Belleforest. It was a mouthful of a name, and, despite the drama and horror yesterday at the funeral, I thought I finally knew what it meant.

Josephine put it well. She, for all her faults, always did know how to resonate with me. *Grief proves your love.*

I would avenge the deaths of my family. That was my purpose.

So I gathered my fencing gear and readied myself for another practice session with Osric.

"Again?" Henri asked between sips of coffee. My friends sat at the small round table whose dark wood stood out sharply against the clinical white of the walls.

"I can't lose," I answered simply.

Julien grunted.

I slipped out, leaving them behind, and was escorted to practice.

Osric waited there, still wearing that absurd red cap. I hadn't seen him without it. He shuffled foot to foot when he saw me, nearly dancing with excitement.

"Good morning, Laertes!" he exclaimed.

A couple other fencing students did step lunges behind him. Two appeared to have finished the warm up and had on their masks. One of them turned. With the mask on, the person was unrecognizable. I could tell from the body language, however, that it was not Hamlet.

"Go on, go on, sir," Osric said, shooing me into the side room where I habitually changed for practice. He looked like a goose trying out a traditional dance.

I nodded and obeyed. The phonograph graced the side table as before; the hooks full of uniforms were the same. Everything seemed untouched since the last time I'd been there with Hamlet. A acrid taste stirred in my stomach. It was nostalgia, bitterness, longing. I didn't know what it was.

Morbid impulse made me set the needle on the record without looking at what it was. Scratching through the horn came the tinkling music of Ravel. I swallowed thickly, turned away, and pulled on my breeches and plastron.

Moments later, after limbering my muscles, I emerged to see a bout in progress. Osric stood to the side, watching the action with a surprisingly keen eye. My limited interaction with the man had made me assume he was foppish or silly. He was, but he was more.

"A hit!" he cried after one of the fencers lunged forward. Postures relaxed, and Osric turned his attention to me. "Laertes, sir, I've matched you with Andreas first."

The others fell back to allow me on the piste. The past few days, my limbs had felt heavier than normal. Even when I wasn't actively dwelling on the horrific losses that had befallen me, my body grieved. The foil seemed twice as heavy.

With Lamord, I didn't always succeed, but I improved, and typically felt charged with life when I practiced. Now, I had nothing but the desire to win. The need to win.

I prepared to start the bout. Osric stood between us a few paces away. My opponent was large but clumsier than I. In less than ten seconds, I scored a hit.

Osric clapped his hands. "Wonderful!" he exclaimed. "I expected to have notes on your footwork, but it was immaculate, sir!"

Lamord would have had notes, but the praise felt good.

"Would you go again, sir?" he asked.

"Yes," I answered uncertainly. A practice was more than a single hit. Why was he asking? I suspected Osric treated me with kid gloves because of recent events. The realization irritated me.

I attacked the next bout with more force, leaning forward, hearing Lamord's voice in my ear, and still earning next contact.

"Ooh!" Osric cooed.

"I should have leaned back," I muttered.

"No such thing. Fencing requires agility of all types. Argal, sometimes it's better to be on the offensive, sir."

His comment took me by surprise. Did he know what I'd planned with the King?

"Argal?" I asked.

"I hear you study Latin." He winked confidentially.

"*Ergo?*" I guessed.

He blanched, but only for a moment. "To mean *therefore*, sir?"

"Yes, and you don't have to call me sir."

"That's kind, I assure you, but as a member of the court, I would prefer it, for my own comfort, if you're amenable, sir." He beamed and touched his hat in a kind of bow without actually bending at the waist.

Andreas looked annoyed, even with his mask on.

"Another?" I prompted.

"Yes, yes! You must prepare for your match with the prince. I hear there has been a great wager placed on your head, sir."

I didn't like the phrasing, but now, as I turned back to my opponent, I imagined Hamlet there. His balance was off, inclining to the right. The angle of the foil invited an attack.

At last, I started to feel alive again.

I won that bout too, took off my mask, and gave a half-smile. Osric's eyes were kind. "By my faith," he said, "I think you must be the best fencer I've laid eyes upon, sir."

Despite the old-fashioned language, his expression revealed utter sincerity.

My smile faded. "Thank you. Have you... seen the prince?"

"No, no, Laertes, sir. I haven't, but I doubt he could best you in any honest contest. You're a true gentleman and a skilled fencer, that much is clear."

I scratched the back of my head sheepishly before replacing my mask. Three hits was hardly enough evidence to make such a conclusion, but Osric's words went down like healing tea. Maybe I was more the man I wanted to become after all.

14

MAY: DEPARTURE

I paced the room, every sinew taut with tension. The match—the killing match—began in half an hour. Hamlet would meet me. I'd see him face to face. I'd get revenge on behalf of my family.

Once, the night before as I slept, I thought I heard the rustle of tattered clothing. Perhaps it was my mother, perhaps not. I had a plethora of ghosts to haunt me now.

Sweat coated my clammy skin. Henri had already left to take his place at the match, since his family's money financed most of the bet on my side. Julien stayed behind, under house arrest in my quarters. His eyes tracked my movements. Perhaps it was my own jumpiness, but Julien hadn't settled either. Neither of us had eaten or drunk anything. Julien hadn't read. I hadn't practiced.

I needed to stretch, to practice footwork. I needed to...

"Calm down, for God's sake!" Julien exclaimed, leaping up.

"I can't! I can't." I shivered, though it wasn't cold.

Julien rested his large hands on my shoulders. "You can."

I focused on his weight on my shoulders and breathed. Perhaps my heart rate slowed. I did feel warmer, which I took as a good sign.

"Or," he continued, more softly now, "you don't have to. I can tell them you're sick. Not even Claudius can force you into this if you've changed your mind."

"No," I replied automatically, backing away from his grip. "No, I'll do it."

I have cause and means and strength and will to do it. But...

I shook my head, dog-like. Undermining thoughts wouldn't help. I had to be sharp, to make my father proud, to do right by Ophelia. The time had come—out of joint, it was true—and I was the only one who could set this right.

Maddening words like *killing* and *murder* kept surfacing like bubbles in my conscience, though.

Now that the moment had come, could I really kill Hamlet?

"I'll back you if you're sure," said Julien.

"I know." My voice came out a whisper. All the times he'd made good on those words returned to me.

I couldn't look at him. Instead, I clambered like a blind man, hardly using my eyes, groping for a comb. Since I disliked pomade and beeswax, I had none to tame my hair. Running the teeth through my unruly waves, my hand shook. That wouldn't do. It had to be steady as an animal stalking its prey.

Julien had his own reasons for wanting Hamlet to stay alive, but I couldn't countenance them. What kind of ruler would he make if he was capable of such erratic violence?

I undid the top button of my dress shirt, then fastened it again. The sweat clinging to my body had soaked through the undershirt and dress shirt both. A jacket would hide it but make my condition worse. A variety of barely-touched dinner jackets hung in my wardrobe. I chose a green herringbone suit of wool tweed and shrugged on first the waistcoat, then the jacket. Father always told me to dress up, and I hadn't listened. Today, I would look the part of a gentleman. God, the suit jacket felt heavy and hot, but I cut a sharp figure in the mirror.

"You aren't going in your fencing uniform?" Julien asked, coming up beside me.

"It's a spectacle," I explained. "The whole royal court will be there.

The King will make his introductions and then we'll prepare to fight." Osric, to whom the King had communicated our plot, had already come to pick up the poisoned blade and the rest of my gear.

An unexpected calm settled on me as I observed myself. Despite my effort to comb it, sandy hair fell over my forehead. The suit I'd chosen was a mix of the stately and professorial. My face looked pale but my eyes gleamed. Despite the smudge of bruises, I was even a little handsome.

"I wish I could be there," said my friend.

Warm gratitude washed over me and I embraced him.

"It's all right. Everyone else will be. And I don't need an audience." I didn't even want one.

We separated and I took one last look in the mirror.

Are not two sparrows sold for a farthing? and one of them shall not fall on the ground without your Father. Fear ye not therefore, ye are of more value than many sparrows.

I sniffed and turned away, a strange mix of settled and chaotic. "I'm as ready as I can be, whatever comes."

All I knew for certain was that all my revenge and all *his* revenge would come to a head and that I just wanted to do my best and be done with it. The future had evaporated with my father. This moment had been the only event I was sure of. Would minutes exist afterward? Was there a future that included me in it?

The notion of walking along the Seine someday ten years from now sounded ludicrous, fossils of an ancient, cherished past. But just as absurd was the idea that Hamlet would rise to the throne of Denmark, reigning over me as king. He would not.

I stretched the neck of my collar and glanced at the clock on the mantle. Seven minutes.

My airways constricted but I kept my center of calm. "I have to go."

Julien gripped my hand in farewell, squeezing harder than was necessary. He was worried for me. I felt it in his rough grasp.

Before exiting, I knocked his cap askew, sending him roaring after me. I fled and shut the door.

Chatter and footsteps floated down the hall. Guards flanked me as I moved stiff as an automaton toward the dueling area, increasing the sensation that I was a man going to execution. Polite applause punctuated the air as I drew nearer.

The piste and other elements had been laid out in on the checkered floor in the throne room itself. I suspected Claudius felt it was apropos. He already sat on the throne with Queen Gertrude beside him, looking pale. Both adorned themselves in finery.

I paused in the doorway. Facing the thrones, Hamlet finished quoting a well-known passage from Plato's *Republic* about the value of sport and exercise in the wise man. He wore a black tailcoat and white bandages on three of his fingers. He hadn't bothered with his hair today, but he did wear a cravat, an antiquated style. I must have left bruises when I throttled him at the funeral. My lip curled in sick satisfaction.

The Queen smiled indulgently at her son as he spread his arms and twirled to address the rest of the small crowd, some thirty or forty. I scanned the people and found Henri standing a little apart from everyone else, graceful and still. He looked at me as though he had tried to catch my eye from the moment I appeared at the threshold.

Hamlet's speech spread out into a commentary on the metaphor he perceived at the center of the passage.

My amusement died and my temper rose at his theatrics. Why did everyone give him the attention he wanted?

That was when the prince noticed me too. "Ah, my abridgement comes," he said, dropping his arms with a smile.

A smile? I didn't understand his mood at all. The last time we spoke, he challenged me at my own sister's funeral, the very sister he'd driven to desperation by killing our father. My chest rose and fell heavily now with labored breaths.

All eyes turned to me. Not only was Henri there, but Osric, Horatio, a woman I recognized from the funeral... I struggled to keep myself under control.

"Come, come!" declared the King, rising and taking hold of Hamlet's hand. He ushered me forward to the center of the room and placed the prince's hand in mine. His bandages rasped against my knuckles. "Let's begin this duel properly."

Hamlet gave me an inscrutable look. "Give me your pardon, sir."

I felt a bit like a cornered animal, the object of all eyes.

"I have done you wrong," Hamlet continued, not letting go of my hand. I wanted to recoil from his touch. "Everyone here knows, and you no doubt have heard, how my mind is afflicted. I never meant to hurt you, but madness got the better of me. We are both victims of it."

At that, I scoffed aloud.

Hamlet wasn't perturbed by my interruption. "Sir," he said, "in front of this audience, be so good as to free me from the accusation of intentional evil." He tilted his head down, almost teasingly. "I know you're generous, Laertes. I never intended to hurt my brother."

That was enough. I pulled my hand back. "I'm satisfied." Premature clapping drowned out some of my next words. "Family honor won't allow me to reconcile with you immediately, I'm sure you know. I need proof of what you say. But until I have it, I'll treat your... professed love as though it's real." I ground my teeth. No words seemed right. I couldn't let the audience know what I was planning, but I couldn't forgive Hamlet on the spot either. As it was, I felt my rageful resolve straining under its own weight.

"Generous!" Hamlet cried, moving apart from me. "What did I say?"

The King climbed to his throne again, linking hands with the Queen. The motion didn't escape Hamlet's notice.

"This is a brother's wager now," he said, more uncertainly, his attention captured by the royal couple. As though rousing from sleep, he inhaled and smiled once more at me. "Let's bring out the foils!"

To great acclamation, Hamlet and I went into separate rooms to change into our white uniforms. My nerveless fingers grappled with the outfit like an enemy. My skin was already slick with sweat and every clasp felt like an impossible challenge. My thoughts in those minutes didn't translate in words so much as impressions, images.

We reemerged, matching creatures who this time barely looked at each other. We stood obediently before the King.

"Set cups of wine on that table," Claudius commanded. "I'll drink to Hamlet! The French claim that Laertes Belleforest is their champion, that no one can best him, but I have wagered that in a dozen bouts, Laertes will not exceed our Prince Hamlet by three hits."

The mostly Danish crowd oohed.

A rack of foils clanked faintly as it rolled out.

"The French have their champion, and we have ours. Now we shall put it to the test. Go, order cannons!"

A servant hustled away to convey the order.

"Come, begin!" the King cried, reaching for one of the goblets placed next to him.

I turned toward the rack of foils. Would I recognize the one I'd doused with poison? Had it gotten lost among the others? The air felt sticky and thick, as in a dream when one cannot move.

Was I really going to do this? I wanted revenge, hot and certain, but... but...

Hamlet already shuffled through the foils, drawing out one and then another. Osric seemed to sense my hesitation because he came forward, red hat and all, and pulled one out for me.

Yes, that was mine. I recognized a nick on the guard.

Did Hamlet see the sheen on the blade? Did he notice the sharp end?

Nausea swirled inside me. I swallowed once, then twice.

"This is too heavy," I found myself saying, trying to hand the blade back to Osric. It truly felt heavier than normal. This time, maybe I could use a normal blade. My mind wouldn't order itself properly.

Osric grinned but his eyes instructed me to keep the foil I already held.

"They're all the same, right?" Hamlet said, weighing his in his hand.

"You don't need a special sword to beat me, do you?" He laughed. "I expect this exhibition will only serve to show off your skills. Next to my ignorance, your expertise will shine."

Women tittered in the audience.

I gave my rapier a couple flicks to channel my unease and frustration. "Are you mocking me?" I growled.

"Of course not."

I would have preferred him to say yes, to berate me, to call me names, to do something so my blood would rise even higher and I'd find the strength to do what I needed to do.

Has he not done enough already?

Osric nodded encouragingly at me, and I trod heavy-footed to the end of the piste.

Hamlet, when he reached the opposite end, turned to address the King. "I think you've laid a wager on the weaker side!" he said, but it was all pandering to the audience. I knew him well enough.

The King's response was shockingly jovial. How was he so calm, so friendly? "I don't fear it. I have seen you both, and the odds are on our side."

I straightened my helmet, more to have something to do with my arms than for any practical purpose, and got in the starting position. Past Hamlet, across from me, Henri's pale face watched me closely. I could see him throughout the match, know he was with me. I tried to steady myself.

"Come on, my lord," I prompted, all this dithering and waiting grinding my determination to powder.

A cannon fired, vibrating through my ribs. I thought I would scream, burst.

"You, the judge," the King said, addressing Osric, "bear a careful eye. And begin!"

I was first to move. My blade flashed forward, but it had poison on it. It could kill Hamlet if it touched him. My muscles recoiled, twitched, unwilling to drive it into him.

Hamlet seized my moment of hesitation and the point of his foil jabbed me in the ribs.

"One!" Hamlet cried.

"No," I said.

"Judgment?" Hamlet looked at Osric.

"A hit. A very palpable hit," the judge said.

The audience clapped.

Stupid hesitation. Why did I hesitate? I hated him. When I looked at him, I saw reflected back the senseless violence he'd caused, the deaths and anguish. I hated him.

"Well, again," I said, preparing.

Lamord would have been proud. I leaned back, letting Hamlet's foil swish past my body, giving me an opening to—

"Another hit!"

"A touch, a touch. I confess it," I ground out.

Hamlet inclined himself toward me. "Shall we—"

"Stay," cried the King.

I startled and looked up.

"Give me the drink," he ordered, reaching out for a new goblet.

No. I can do it. But I didn't have the benefit of my expression to assuage him. I wasn't weak. I wasn't vacillating. I had to be the one to take revenge, not the King and his damned drink.

Before I could think of a way to communicate that, he had already sent the wine to Hamlet on a plated salver.

"There's to your health," said Claudius, lifting his chin in invitation.

I could imagine Hamlet's expression well enough as he paused, looking at the cup. His posture relaxed and he returned his attention to me. "I'll play this bout first," he said. "Set it aside for now."

The servant carrying the tray obeyed.

The King betrayed nothing of his disappointment.

Once again, we prepared to fence.

"Wait, if you won't drink..." The Queen rose and snatched the cup from the tray.

The King rose, his own drink in his hand.

She wouldn't, would she? My gaze darted between the two of them, but what could I say? The King would stop her.

I couldn't think that way. I had to save her, had to prevent her from taking that drink. I left the piste and approached the thrones.

She walked past me down to Hamlet, who drew off his helmet to embrace her.

"Our son shall win!" she declared, brandishing the poison. "You're out of breath, my darling. Let me wipe your face." She provided a handkerchief from somewhere and drew it across his brow.

Hamlet acted falsely affronted, but was clearly enjoying her attention.

"If you won't drink, then I will," she said. "The Queen carouses to your good fortune!"

"Hear!" cried someone in the crowd, unaware of the thread that separated us all from calamity.

"Madame!" I yelled as she raised the cup to her lips.

"Gertrude!" the King shouted over me. "Don't drink yet."

What followed happened slowly. The Queen stood in the exact center of a white tile. Hamlet, beside her, stood on a black one. *She can move anywhere she likes,* I thought crazily. Perhaps the onlookers were the pawns in this chess game.

The Queen's gaze trailed from the King to me to the cup to Hamlet. She aged before my eyes, and in that moment, I knew she understood everything. Her look frightened me.

"I will, my lord," she said, aiming the veneer of a smile at the assembly. "I pray you pardon me."

Before I could move away from the thrones, she had tipped back the cup and her throat flexed with the drink. My heart stopped, all functions pausing in united horror.

The King bent toward me. "That's..."

I nodded, cut him off.

Hamlet acted blithely unaware. He was no fool. How could he not see his world cracking from within?

Now with new desperation, the Queen stepped toward her son.

"Let me wipe your face," she said again, lifting the handkerchief still in her hand. Hamlet leaned in as though to get his mother's care over with sooner.

The King had frozen, watching his wife drink the poison he'd prepared.

"I'll hit him now," I whispered.

"I don't think so," Claudius replied.

I didn't argue with him. Whether he disbelieved in my abilities or simply had given up because of the Queen's actions, I couldn't contradict him. This act was against my conscience and conscience made me cowardly. Its loud voice drove away even my hot anger.

"Come on for the third, Laertes!" Hamlet cried, helmet still off. "Stop dallying over there. I'm afraid you're spoiling me with all these easy fights."

That was enough to galvanize me into motion. "I'll show you an easy fight!"

The Queen moved ponderously back toward her throne, leaving me room to jump in and attack with my foil. Hamlet defended himself, and laughed with victory. My actions grew more frantic, my attacks less calculated and more predatory.

This man, this smug prince, was no friend of mine. I was Laertes Belleforest, son of Polonius, and I craved revenge.

"Nothing either way," came Osric's voice.

Hamlet's foil kept mine at bay. I knew I wasn't playing my best, but I could hardly control my limbs. All my being strained forward in attack. I didn't let him get another hit, but neither did I touch him with my foil.

I realized dimly we were off the piste. Someone shouted as we edged toward the crowd. I kept slashing and advancing, aiming for skin.

Hamlet tripped over his feet. His stumble gave me the opening.

I cut him across the face, drawing a red line of poisoned blood across his cheek. Vicious satisfaction welled in me. The crowd gasped.

Hamlet's expression morphed into something monstrous. I saw it all there. He couldn't believe what I had done, that I would hurt him, that I had won. With a shout, he rushed me, sending us crashing to the hard floor.

I let go of the blade as we grappled so that I didn't accidentally cut myself or anyone else with it. Hamlet tore off my helmet, catching my chin with its edge and forcing my head back painfully. A bead of his blood fell on my face and I spat.

All the energy I'd felt twisting my body and heart these past weeks exploded out. I didn't care for injury. I didn't care who saw. We were creatures, not men, at that moment.

When I came to, Henri and Osric held my arms. Warm blood coated my ear. A few steps away, Horatio held Hamlet back. In Hamlet's hand dangled the bloody sword.

I touched the side of my head, looked at the foil. The cartilage of my ear had been sliced by a sharp blade. My blade. The poisoned one.

"Are you all right?" Horatio asked Hamlet, squaring him up to take a closer look. He wiped some of the dripping blood from Hamlet's face.

"Laertes. Laertes!"

I turned dully, uncomprehending.

Henri's dark eyes were close to mine. "Laertes?" he said again.

But we both knew.

"Oh! The Queen!" Osric exclaimed, pointing. The Queen lay on the ground, dark red dress spilling out from where she fell.

Hamlet extricated himself from Horatio's grasp. "How is the Queen?" He trotted toward the thrones, where Queen Gertrude had fallen.

The King tried to step in front of him. "She swoons to see you bleed. Please give her a moment."

The lines in her forehead deepened, growing dark against pale skin. Gertrude's eyes rolled as the poison took hold, but when she could control their movements, they pleaded up at her son. Hamlet couldn't fall for the King's blatant lie.

"The drink," the Queen said, hardly more than a croaking whisper.

His eyes grew wide as a wild horse's, obviously trying to take this in, to make it into something that made sense. But it didn't. Hamlet fell to his knees beside his mother and took her hand in his. The curve of his spine spoke of a broken child. Single-minded horror drowned his usual effervescence, muted it to a painting.

"Get away from her. She's fine," Claudius insisted.

My heart twisted. The Queen was dying. I could count the number of her remaining words. And then there would be no more. Her final words to Hamlet hung on her lips, but she couldn't get them out. I felt them in my own chest, the unspoken words of my own mother.

"The drink," she tried again, wringing Hamlet's hand. "Oh, Hamlet!" Tears streaked her cheeks.

Hamlet grabbed hold of her as though to drag her from the next life into this one.

Her head, heavy, bent to the floor. "I am poisoned." Her eyes rolled and stopped.

Exclamations erupted all around the space. Heads swiveled for exits. Disbelieving murmurs coated my bloody ears, and Henri all but held me upright.

Deadly cold was spreading from my neck down my spine.

Hamlet pulled Gertrude's lifeless body into his lap. Not enough. It was never enough. I knew.

"Treason!" he finally called out, looking up at Claudius. "Lock the doors. Let no one in or out!" His thumb absently played with his mother's hair, but blood was on it, so her temples reddened at his touch.

"You heard him," said the King. "Lock the doors! We'll find out what happened here." His tone commanded allegiance, but his eyes had gone dark. Servants and guards flew to obey.

Hamlet hadn't risen from his mother's side. In his grief I saw the portraiture of mine. His sins were many and they were terrible, but I could spare him the guilt I knew so intimately of blaming himself for his mother's death.

"The King!" I said, words bursting as though through a barrier. "The King's to blame."

All the audience moved as if they were trapped in a collapsing room, desperate to get out. Even Osric left my side to perform some service. Dresses and suits striped my view of the royal family. I think Claudius was trying to get someone's attention to silence me.

"No," Henri whispered.

But I had to go on. "Your mother's poisoned. And... Hamlet..." Blank terror at my confession seized me. "And... so are you."

Someone gasped, maybe the Italian.

I tried to swallow against my dry throat. Such an odd confessional, a murderer to his victim. I didn't regret killing the part of him that ruined my life, but he wore masks too, and I loved some of them deeply.

Hamlet rose, his bleeding face almost exultant. His mother lay at his feet.

"The sword and the drink were poisoned," I explained, almost my entire weight depending on Henri now. "Neither of us have half an hour."

At that, Henri made a strangled sound and dropped me accidentally. I flinched as my elbows caught the stone floor.

In that moment, Hamlet sprinted clumsily to where he'd dropped my blade. Was poison polluting his mind already? Henri spread himself over me as Hamlet stormed toward us. I felt Henri grip my uniform. Then Hamlet passed.

"Here," Hamlet cried, rushing at the King. "The point envenomed too?" The flash of a blade, a clamber for the cup. "Then die, and drink this, you incestuous murderer! Follow my mother!"

I couldn't see very well what happened between Hamlet and the King. Henri wouldn't get off me until it was all over. I could just make out Hamlet's white shoes nearly pressed against the King's, as though he were holding him there to stab him with the poisoned foil. More screams, and then something red fell on Hamlet's uniform. I couldn't tell if it was wine or blood. More of the King's body came into view as he convulsively slumped to the ground.

Slowly, Henri's weight lifted. He must have perceived the threat to have passed. It hadn't, though. It was within me.

Claudius lay at the foot of his throne and Hamlet stood like an avenging god above two bodies. The image pierced my confused brain and lodged there. He had avenged his own father and he had loved his mother.

Even though she died in his arms, he couldn't save her. The thought swirled and swirled, searching for purchase inside me. He wasn't to blame for her death.

In the heightened chaos that followed, Henri bent over me. "What can I get you? What can I do? You'll be all right," he said.

Hot tears stung my eyes. I shook my head.

"No, you'll be all right." He slicked off some of the blood near my ear with a finger and flicked it away in disgusted helplessness.

"There's nothing."

I thought of Ophelia's compassion, Julien's dreams of becoming a professor, Henri's reckless love, Father's loyalty and love of words. And suddenly, to be made of pieces of those I loved seemed a privilege, not a cage. I wish I had known it sooner.

Convulsively, I tried to kick my leg. Panic threaded like lightning as it didn't move. Kick, kick. Like something from a nightmare, it lay, a corpse attached to me, dead flesh. Watching my still leg was like watching a sad play—sad, but ultimately unconnected to me. I missed it like I would a beloved character.

Henri started to cry.

"Would you... lift me up?" I asked. My tongue had grown heavy in my mouth.

Time ticked away. I wouldn't spend it in silence. "Hamlet," I said, too quietly. I was always repeating myself. "Hamlet!"

The prince finally heard and walked heavily toward me. Guards, hesitant to arrest him while he still held the poisoned sword, gave him a wide berth.

"Claudius... killed your father." I meant it as a question but we both knew the truth.

"Yes."

"Then that was... just."

A flicker in his eye meant he also remembered that one night when he'd said the same to me. I knew in that moment what I had to do. Looking at Hamlet's bloodied face, I finally understood. All those years I'd harbored so much shame, but forgiveness could reach even me. I was not responsible for my mother's death, and if I could have this last piece, then I could finally forgive myself.

"We're both sinners," I began, gasping on the last word almost in a laugh. "So... Hamlet, exchange forgiveness with me. I don't blame you for my death. And... forgive me for yours."

Hamlet stumbled, fell. His friend Horatio flew to his side.

I waited. My vision blurred.

Perhaps it was foolish to exchange forgiveness with this unstable prince. Julien—ah, Julien!—would reprimand me for it. Ophelia would praise me. Henri remained silent, but he kept propping up my head.

Something profound passed between us when we locked eyes again, the gravity of two dying men with only final words.

"May heaven make you free of it," Hamlet said.

And I was.

Dying is not what many people think. It's confusing and terrifying. Worse than death itself. I knew it was happening, but I refused to fully believe it. No one expects to stop breathing, not really. But now I was ready, as ready as I could be, and readiness was all.

Voices spoke in the darkness that enveloped me. I heard Henri humming as he drew and Julien speaking Latin. I heard my father's admonishments and Ophelia's laugh. I heard Josephine singing and my mother telling stories. I heard Hamlet saying words words words. They clamored for me to listen to them because there was no time and I was falling asleep but I shouldn't and I couldn't remember why.

The rest was silence.

For a while.

Henri's sketch of me has pride of place in his new home. Julien, the next year, earned top marks on his exams and bought The Battlements himself. Dynasties shifted in Denmark.

I didn't expect this story to be told so many times in so many different, incomplete ways, but I'm glad that people remember Ophelia's name and my father's name.

And now, here I am with you, because you needed to know the truth. Visitations, I've learned, are often about telling the real story so that it can live on.

Perhaps that is why I felt compelled to tell you everything. I didn't know which part of my tale you needed to hear, so I gave it all, even the parts least flattering to myself. I'm forbidden to talk about *after*, so I won't.

Mark this, though, when I look back at everything—the silver cigarette case, the amber opera house, the skull on the mantel, the cups of coffee and the late nights—simply to be is vastly beautiful.

AUTHOR'S NOTE

Know, first of all, that this is a work of love.

As I'm writing this, I have loved Shakespeare's *Hamlet* for fifteen years and taught it for ten. I've read it countless times and was thrilled to find new aspects as I was researching this book.

Laertes always struck me as a criminally underrated character. Famously, he's Hamlet's foil. He goes through similar experiences—losing his father to murder and looking to avenge him, besides claiming to care about the same woman (though in different ways) and having a similar skill set, age, and cultural background—but he deals with these things in a nobler way.

Instead of lollygagging about righting a profound wrong, he rushes in to confront the person he assumes is his father's murderer. Instead of shouting at Ophelia for making decisions he doesn't agree with, he suggests she leave Hamlet so she doesn't get hurt. When faced with the truth that he has murdered his friends, Hamlet responds, "They are not near my conscience" (5.2.58). Laertes, on the other hand, as he prepares to kill his father's murderer, mutters, "[It] is almost 'gainst my conscience" (5.2.282).

Laertes is not a perfect character. He suffers from serious vices and difficulties like almost all of Shakespeare's characters, but I think his position as the man Hamlet could have been if he were *better* has so far been overlooked. I've never seen or heard a Laertes that did real justice to the character, at least as I viewed him. So that's why I wrote this book. I wanted to explore the story further through the eyes of someone I've long cared about and the world has ignored.

To make this book more cohesive, I intentionally ignored some passages from the play. Hamlet and Laertes, for example, are university age here, despite the play pegging Hamlet at thirty. Every other indication suggests he's closer to twenty, so that's what I chose.

Other differences are not a result of ignoring the original text, but having to account for it. Where did Laertes get the poison for the sword? Why does Polonius tell Reynaldo not to lay "another scandal" on Laertes? (2.1.29) Obviously, since Laertes is in France for the majority of the action, I had to get creative. Hence, the new characters and events that Shakespeare didn't invent.

The time period was another consideration. Shakespeare's action seems to take place in a fantasy version of his own time, even with references to contemporary phenomena, such as the popularity of boys' choirs eating into theatre profits (see 2.2). I thought about setting this story in roughly the 1600's too, but I wanted the story to feel more modern. I'll gladly admit I was going for a dark academia aesthetic, which required a time not perfectly contemporary, but close. So, the 1920's it was. The more I researched and thought about it, this decade seemed like the perfect backdrop to the story I wanted to tell. Shakespeare did the same thing with his sources, so I don't feel bad. I think I have his blessing.

I've striven to keep the core themes intact, of life and death, action and thought, perception and reality. With adaptations, respecting the heart of the story is the most important thing a person can do. At least, I think so.

That meant dealing with difficult topics like mental illness and suicide. A quick online search will show many free hotlines and text numbers for anyone struggling with thoughts of self-harm. Please reach out if you are battling depression or suicidal ideation. You have a right to exist, and that existence is meaningful even if it's messy, so please fight for yourself.

I hope this story brings new fans to Shakespeare's play and brings it to life in new ways for long-time lovers of the story. I certainly enjoyed playing with the language, ideas, and characters to find a new voice for *Hamlet* (or should I say *Laertes?*)

ACKNOWLEDGMENTS

To those who studied *Hamlet* with me, who came up with conspiracy theories about Gertrude's guilt, who flopped dramatically on the floor, who performed soliloquies with honest conviction, who told David Tennant that Hamlet was his best work, who read the Player King with an "old man voice", who wrote moving essays about Hamlet's silence, thank you. Teaching you has been one of the greatest joys of my life.

Many people helped with making this book, from my writing group (Ed, Debbie, and Amanda—you are wonderful!) to Frederik Virklund and Laura Kiel, the lovely people at Kronborg Castle who graciously answered my questions. I was inspired and encouraged by Nicole Galland and Dr. John Freeh. Luke Monson, Julien-like, confirmed my Latin. Elizabeth Vietor lent suggestions about Classics that I wouldn't have considered on my own. My beta readers asked probing questions, pointed out problems, and made me believe this story worked Thank you particularly to Quinn, Summer, Lily, Elizabeth, Carolyn, Rachel, and Syd.

The primary versions of *Hamlet* I consulted were the editions edited by A.R. Braunmuller and Burton Raffel, respectively.

QUESTIONS FOR DISCUSSION

1.	In what ways does the first scene foreshadow the last scene? How does Laertes' relationship with Hamlet change?

2.	Laertes feels like he can be himself with friends in Paris but not in with his family in Denmark. Where and with whom do you feel most yourself? Why?

3.	In Shakespeare's *Hamlet*, it's an open question whether or not the Ghost exists. Do you think the ghost of Laertes' mother is real or a figment of his imagination? Does it matter?

4.	Josephine is an ambiguous character. To what degree is she a positive influence on Laertes and to what degree is she a negative influence?

5.	The Battlement boys all study Classics. What is one of your favorite things to study? Why?

6.	Laertes notes that Ophelia doesn't "seem oppressed" as a woman. What are some ways that you can recognize a marginalized group of people and help to rectify the issue?

7.	Is revenge ever justified, or is it always wrong?

8.	Loss is a major theme in this story. How do each of the characters deal with loss? Are those reactions and coping mechanisms healthy or destructive? What are some of the best ways to help ourselves and each other deal with great loss?

9.	At the end of the story, Laertes says, "I didn't know which part of my tale you needed to hear, so I gave it all." What do you feel like you needed to take away?

10. So much of this novel is about appreciating the beauty of your own life. What are some of the small, beautiful elements of your life right now?

⚜

Reach out to the author at carly@carly-stevens.com. She'd love to know what you thought of *Laertes* and might even join your discussion virtually!